WHITE RABBIT

WHITE RABBIT
K. A. Laity

www.foxspirit.co.uk

Cover Art by S.L.Johnson

typesetting and conversion by handebooks.co.uk

ISBN: 978-1-909348-47-9 epub
ISBN: 978-1-909348-48-6 mobi
ISBN: 978-1-909348-49-3 paperback

A Fox Spirit Original
Fox Spirit Books
www.foxspirit.co.uk
adele@foxspirit.co.uk

for Mr B
who lured me into crime
like a stranger with candy

'A journey is an hallucination.' ~ De Selby

I was logging some mileage in the luminiferous ether when an urgent knocking derailed my concentration. Cursing Jinx's name—he ought to know better by now—I tried to ignore the hammering, but I was already back-pedalling in weird space and falling up the rabbit hole into the blinking light.

'Nothing?' My client, a wan young man of indeterminate age, looked displeased but unsurprised. Such low expectations deserved disappointment.

'Apologies for the interruption,' I murmured, getting up and crossing to the door where my protégé continued to pound with insane enthusiasm. I jerked it open, catching his fist in mid-air and twisting it sharply.

He whimpered.

'I'm with a client,' I said through clenched teeth, shoving his hand away from me. 'What have we said about interrupting me with clients?' I turned around to smile at the pale young man with the doughy face. 'I don't want to be interrupted. Each client is important.'

Jinx winced. Then he leaned forward to indicate we were to confer privately. The effect would have been improved had his breath not stunk of the cheap kidney pie he'd consumed earlier, or if his pasty white face did not resemble an emotionally-stunted panda's second cousin. I could have done without his presence altogether at that moment. Then he handed me the scrawled note that would change my life.

In his untidy slant appeared the words, 'Peaches Dockmuir.'

If I'd been a Tex Avery cartoon character my eyes would have bulged, made the a-whoo-gah horn blare and then the clanking sound of a till opening its drawer and coins spewing out onto the floor. 'I'm so very sorry, Mr Toynbee,' I said turning back to my morose client, 'but something of an emergency has come up, I'm afraid. Please see my colleague to rebook our appointment. No charge, of course.' I hated to pronounce those words, but better one hare ran free today than buckshot frighten the lot of them.

Toynbee stirred, gathering his belongings about him. Why should anyone under the age of fifty require so much paraphernalia just to amble about town? 'I am gravely disappointed with our session, Mr. Draygo.'

'As am I,' I agreed, trying not too inelegantly to give him the heave-ho. 'We shall have to try again when the planets are more propitious.' What absolute twaddle. I knew Jinx would book him for Thursday week.

Short of shoving him out the door myself, there wasn't much I could do to get Toynbee on his way, but at last he did. I ran around the room relighting the candles that had gone out while I tried to contain my excitement.

Peaches Dockmuir! If you're going to run a fly-by-night psychic organisation inherited from your late Auntie Vera, then you need a client like an über-trashy trophy wife from the provinces like Peaches—all glitz, tacky glamour and spend-thrift ways with a bottle tan to boot. The tabloids splashed her bovine features across the pages weighed down with bling as she jet-setted from hither and yon. I could almost feel the gold jingling into my pockets.

I hadn't tasted that kind of dosh since I left the life behind. Given my weakness I'd since thought of turning to the chemical trade in order to return my books to solvency, but considering how many former colleagues were panting for my blood, signs pointed away from that path, as we say in the trade. Bitter bloody bores, policemen are. Nonetheless it had been for the best, as I doubtless would have become my own best customer all too soon. Call it a premonition if you must.

Fortunately I hadn't overindulged this day as my golden goose waltzed through the door. Peaches looked rather golden too, or was it just her leathery tan? No, there was some kind of sparkle dust on her cheeks that lent credence to the golden girl rep. She danced in like a pasha, trailing a scent of fruit and an entourage.

'Welcome, Ms. Dockmuir,' I said gravely, hoping I wasn't

overplaying my hand with obsequiousness. I had so seldom made any effort at all to interact with my fellow humans of late that every gesture seemed a parody of politeness, though I stopped short of actually bowing. 'Wouldn't you feel more comfortable with a little more privacy?'

'I'm not Dockmuir anymore!' She whipped off her sunglasses to reveal eyes so thickly rimmed with kohl as to make the shades superfluous. 'I'm divorcing that rat bastard and taking back my own name.'

'Which is?' I asked nonplussed.

'Weiner.'

Peaches Weiner. It sounded like a cheap barbecue recipe. I smothered the giggle that wanted to escape my mouth. Maybe I had ingested a little more fairy dust than I thought or maybe it was just the incongruence of her chavtastic look and that utter humourlessness. Say what you will of the *demi-monde*, they know how to have a laugh. 'Well, sit yourself down if you please, but I ask again: wouldn't you like a little more privacy? Most of our clients prefer some solitude to commune with spirits and reflect upon the messages from beyond.' God, listen to the rusty creaks in that speech. Had so little changed from Blavatsky's time? Remind me to hire a carnival barker to scrounge some new patter.

'Oi, my cousin Marybelle said you weren't no fraud, so I'm here, but I don't need the mumbo jumbo, hear?' She pointed a shiny manicured nail at me as if she were well accustomed to putting the tradesmen in their place. 'And I can't get rid of them,' she added, jerking a thumb at the scruffs and looking displeased and oddly uncomfortable. 'Until the lawyers sort out the details I'm not allowed to go anywhere alone.'

I looked at the phalanx of security drones in black tees and trousers. 'They follow you into the loo?'

'They do.' She made a face. 'Disgusting, innit?'

I almost felt sorry for her. There are places a person really needs to be alone.

'I have doubled up on the cheap curries in their honour,' she said with a triumphant smile. In that glossy rictus I could see why a man like Dockmuir might fall for her moxie.

The heavies remained statues but I could sense a seething resentment.

'What can I assist you with?' I asked all Jeeves-like as we settled around the oak. Auntie Vera's patented séance table offered old world comforts with new world tech. Too soon for the whole razzmatazz, but it always gave comfort to have it in reserve.

I don't know what I was expecting—her sainted mum or a departed pooch—but Peaches flummoxed me by saying, 'I want to talk to the late Mrs. Dockmuir.'

Unexpected that. When in doubt, fall back on the script. 'Have you, er, got something of hers I can use as an anchor?'

'I got her man, ain't I?' Peaches laughed like a hyena. Normally when people say that, you imagine they are erring somewhat to the side of truth. This was not the case.

'Indeed,' I agreed all friendly like, noticing that the entourage did not share her mirth. Dour to a fault they were. 'But I was hoping for something tangible that I could use to make the—ah—connection.'

'Right.' Peaches upended her doubtless expensive handbag on the table and rifled through the contents. I was pleased to see a tiny derringer with shiny pearl handle grips. Somehow that sealed the image of the gangster's moll that she had been born to be. 'Here, how's this? Was hers before.'

She tossed me a long wallet or check holder thing emblazoned with the Coach name so I knew it was posh (hey, I've read magazines at the dentist's too). I held it a minute for show, then nodded gravely. 'I think this will do.'

Jinx had already gone around and relit the joss sticks and now brought the lights down with a slow turn of the knob. Ah, the infinite uses of a dimmer switch, the psychic's best friend. The posse shifted a bit uncomfortably. Let them. Out of their comfort zone and into mine.

I learned it from the best.

Auntie Vera taught me as a teen, the eternal Woodbine dangling from the side of her lipsticked mouth. 'It's 50 per cent sideshow and 50 per cent intuition,' she'd always say as she swapped out the candle butts for fresh tapers. 'You keep it on that even keel, you keep it paying. Most people so anxious to know the answers they tell 'em to you. But don't neglect the show or they'll suss it out. Everybody wants to believe.'

So I made a show of getting into the mind set which was mostly a lot of practiced gestures. The fading spark of fairy dust in my veins made me eager to replenish it, but with all things considered, now wasn't the time. I'd have to actually use my own grey cells—just think of the gravy train that had pulled up at my door, I reminded my addled brain, that should be inspiration enough. Yee doggies, as the Duke might say.

'Do you know her Christian name?'

'Her what?' Peaches looked at me, mouth agape.

'Her first name.'

She snickered. 'I thought you meant what name she was baptised under. How should I know, I wasn't there. But her name was Beryl.'

'How unfortunate.' I closed my eyes and rolled my head around a little as I flexed my shoulders. I held the wallet between my hands, caressing the smooth leather. 'I call forth the spirit of Beryl Dockmuir, whose wallet this was. Come forth and approach us if your spirit be willing.' I have dulcet tones, my auntie always said, smooth as this hand tooled leather in my hands. Rich folk do have nice things.

'Do I need to chant or summat?' Peaches inquired, putting me off my rhythm.

'No,' I said with a strained smile. 'Just stay silent and be receptive.' I repeated my call to the spirit of Beryl if it be willing, rolling my head around gently as if pinging the strands of the luminous. 'Is that you, Beryl?' I asked when the time seemed propitious. 'I am sorry, Mrs. Dockmuir. I didn't mean to be so familiar.'

'Can I ask her something?' Peaches said, a little too eagerly.

'Oh, she's drawn back. Is there a shadow between you?'

'Well, yeah,' Peaches snorted. 'I was screwing her husband behind her back three nights a week before she died. She might resent that a wee bit.'

'Indeed. She's reluctant to speak with you.' Let's mine it

for all we can, eh? I could see stretching this out for weeks maybe.

'If you're trying to drive the price up,' Peaches said, all too quickly, 'don't worry about it. I brought cash with me. Just ask her.'

Ca-ching! There's a lot to be said for the quick score, too. 'What is it you'd like to ask of the deceased?'

'I want to ask her about the white rabbit.' Peaches looked uncharacteristically grim. So did the posse behind her. Well, they had looked impassive before, but I could feel an undercurrent of tension that hadn't been there before. Yes, I do have my moments.

'The white rabbit?'

'Yeah, she ought to know. I mean I think she will.'

I closed my eyes again. 'Mrs. Dockmuir, draw near to us again. We have an urgent question to beg of you. Please Mrs. Dockmuir, draw near—'

'If she wants anything I can give her—I mean, I can say sorry about the old man,' Peaches rushed to offer. 'He turned out to be a right bastard and it were only a bit of fun and, well, I'd say more but they're here.' She jerked her head at the crew spread out behind her chair, their black shapes in the darkness like standing stones.

'Mrs. Dockmuir, can you forgive Peaches for her transgressions?' I mouthed the words with holy vowels, grooving on the absurdity. I could dine on this story for months, if only I had friends to dine with.

'Is she forgiving me?'

'Her mien looks more kindly.'

'Her what?'

'Her expression. Draw near, Mrs. Dockmuir. We have an urgent question for you.' The room hummed with tense anticipation. Even the stone faces must be catching the spirit, so to speak. I might not know much about art, but I know when I've got a room in the palm of my hand. I started to believe it myself.

'Is she here?' Peaches asked, nearly breathless.

'She is near,' I said in my best James Mason voice.

'Sorry about the old man,' Peaches said, a hint of genuine feeling softening her tone. 'I can't say it wasn't worth it, but he was a shit to you and to me as well. We know what he really cares about, innit so?'

'She's nodding.'

'Does she forgive me?'

I shrug. 'She cannot be responsible for your soul. But she doesn't hold a grudge.'

'Fair enough.' Peaches leaned forward. 'All right, serious now. I got a question.'

I closed my eyes again. 'Mrs. Dockmuir, the querent addresses you.'

'I gotta know, Mrs. D, what's the truth? I found the white rabbit and I know that the money from it—'

CRACK.

I opened my eyes. Peaches had collapsed onto the table top. A faint cloud of smoke wafted over her. One of the crew in black leaned forward to slide a pistol across the table toward me and I stopped its spin, gaping at the group of them as they silently exited the room.

I stared at Peaches. She wasn't breathing. I looked down at the gun in my hand, the smell of blood and gunpowder in my nose and thought only,

Fuck me.

'Explain it to me again,' Coburn said, revelling in the interrogation. He had one eyebrow cocked as he exhaled the words and some smoke with what seemed like infinite patience if it weren't for that raised brow, which suggested that every word you'd said he considered to be entirely dubious. A technique meant to unsettle the guilty. It wouldn't work on me for two reasons.

First, I wasn't guilty of anything but being a chump for those faceless heavies.

Second, I had been his partner and I knew all about his golden technique. 'I told you already, Coburn. Get those goons back here and I'll help you work them over until they spill which one of them was the one who done it.' My arrogance petered out by the end of the sentence as I realised I was deep in the poo, as Auntie Vera would say.

'So you don't know which one of them you're accusing of murder?' Coburn's brow had packed its bags for the Arctic Circle apparently. 'Handy that.'

'They were all alike in their similitude.' Sweat began to ooze from various folds of my flesh. 'Do you really think I'd stoop so low and so stupidly?'

Wrong question. 'I wouldn't be surprised by any stupidity you came up with, Draygo.' Coburn sniffed. It might have been the beginnings of hay fever. Or a late winter cold. Probably it was just his contempt for me and my hedonistic downward spiral.

Speaking of which, I could use a little more dust in my veins now that the adrenaline had departed. Once again however, the time did not seem to be propitious. 'Ask Jinxy here,' I said, cocking a thumb over my shoulder at my faithful dogsbody. He was too bone-headed to lie and Coburn knew that.

'We have asked Jinx. Your man claims not to be in the room when it happened.' Coburn smiled. It wasn't a cheery sight. 'Not looking good for you, Jawbone.'

I winced. That's the thing about a nickname. You think you'd grow out of it over time, but it just digs in like a tick, burrowing under your skin. Or whatever it is that burrows under your skin. I thought it was a tick. 'I didn't shoot her. You have to haul in those neckless wonders. I know the prints on the gun are mine and all, but—'

There was a commotion at the door as they brought out the still body of Peaches Dockmuir née Weiner. I felt bad for her. Sure, she had been tacky and trashy and common as muck, but surely she didn't deserve to be cracked dead at my table. Nor to leave me in the muck as it were, saddled with the suspicion of guilt for offing her.

'We're going to have to take you down to the station,' Coburn said. 'You know the drill.'

'Jinx, lock up behind me, all right?' I called over my shoulder as Coburn slapped the bracelets on. I looked up at him with a sour taste in my mouth. 'I take it there are press outside?'

'Not unless someone tipped 'em off.' His grin had more than a hint of cruelty. As we elbowed out the door a sea of flashing lights greeted us. There was no use trying to hide my face, so I tried to look as innocent as possible, which is hard to do when all those cameras are going off and the scribes of the nation are screaming, 'Why'd you do it?! What were Peaches' last words?!'

Coburn shoved me into the back seat of the patrol car with those questions unanswered. I saw Jinx hastily heaving the door closed against the persistent efforts of the seasoned paps and—incongruously—a ginger cat. My old friend's face was pinched with horror. Poor guy. He wasn't used to this kind of attention anymore. I'd gladly trade places with him.

At the station house I met more of my former colleagues, who made their displeasure known. Not to say that anyone spat in my face—I'm sure it was just a particularly heavy foggy morning dew (in the late afternoon) and as it was raining, it had to be expected—but I got booked in record time, printed and tossed into a holding cell without losing any teeth.

Doubtless Mr. Dockmuir himself reckoned matters would be handled swiftly. It's what he paid for after all. I looked around the cell, wishing I'd had quieter quarters as the itch had begun to whisper under my skin. Half a dozen other folks in transit joined me: two drunks just past the belligerent point and beginning to settle into remorse, a cagey looking hood who glared at everyone but kept to himself, a guy with the self-righteous look of a thief and an old vagabond who kept humming a Wanda Jackson tune under his breath.

I needed to think. I needed some dust. I wanted to get out of there and rewind the last hour or so before the itch got too much and I couldn't see things clearly anymore. None of that was going to happen though. I expected I could get sprung before too long, but it might take overnight depending on the circumstances. Poor Jinx probably had been well spooked and that might make him forgetful; doubtless he would get around to calling my legal rep eventually.

Eventually.

The oldster kept singing about going down down down and how he was gonna get me someday—or get someone someday. I suppose I didn't need to take it personally but it began to grate like sandpaper on my thoughts. I needed to calm myself. The cacophony of the cell hammered me like a nun's ruler—not enough to really hurt, but it kept my thoughts scrambled. My nerves shredded like cheap plastic carrier bags.

Right, I was better than this. Calm thoughts, deep breaths, no wishing I had a little powder to course through my veins and put all right with the world. No. I shuffled back across the cell, looking for a spot to sit down. I steered well clear of the drunks: too unpredictable. The old tramp kept muttering and singing tunelessly, eyes closed, looking almost beatific. He irritated me even more with his peaceful look.

I finally leaned in the corner, pulling my brain waves around me like a cloak. Tried to get my mind off spinning and getting weak in the knees and going deep as the old man sang. I had to release the golden goose that I thought Peaches would be and remember. My imaginings had crept onto a shiny golden carpet and taken wing. They needed to come back down to earth.

I tried to picture the phalanx of security folk radiating forth from the figure of Peaches. I closed my eyes but it did no good. Squat, muscular, clad alike in black tee shirts and jeans. There might even have been a woman among them, I couldn't be sure. That's the problem with real security; they aren't just there for show. They're a weapon, cocked and ready like a pistol in shoulder holster, poised for action whenever needed.

Speaking of which, there was the gun with my prints on it. The ever-popular Smith & Wesson, little altered from its 19th century grandparent—a reliable handgun in a small package. Surely it could be traced back to Dockmuir and his posse of security clones.

Or could it?

Sweat broke out on my brow and it wasn't just the jonesing now. Would he have been paranoid enough to cover his tracks in advance? Because wasn't this his doing ultimately? The men (and maybe one woman) in black were really just part of the trigger. He had concerns enough to monitor her. He knew that she was leaving even if she hadn't said it outright to him.

Then again, it was Peaches. She doubtless pointed a manicured nail at him and told him what a shit he had been and how she was going to get herself a lawyer that could undo that pre-nup.

Murder: so much cheaper than legal rep.

I got up to pace around again. I didn't care if it made me look suspicious. Who was going to say a word about it? The tramp continued to sing Wanda tunelessly, the hood continued to glare. The drunks had nodded off. We might be monitored but that was the least of my worries.

Peaches Dockmuir might be the tackiest nouveau rich trophy wife around but she was also the most famous. And she'd been shot dead in my place while my eyes were closed with a gun now conveniently adorned with my prints.

Face it, Draygo, my gibbering, paranoid insect shadow argued, *you were set up!*

I took a few turns about the cell, trying not to speed my steps too much, but the jittery feeling travelled from my brain to my extremities and brought back some adrenaline with it. Which helped—don't get me wrong. Any drug in a pinch, I always say. But it wasn't conducive to quiet contemplation and reason. Down down down, I hummed along with the old tramp. Down the memory lane back to the moment where it all went pear-shaped.

What was it Peaches had said just before they plugged her? Something about a rabbit? I had assumed it had to do with failing a pregnancy test. Maybe it was something more. I mean, does anybody use that figure of speech anymore? My Auntie Vera would say that with derision when her any of her apprentice mediums disappeared. 'The rabbit died, my son. So she's hopped it.'

Did Peaches leave him because she was pregnant? Or did she leave him and then find she was pregnant? Or claimed she was and wasn't? Or—

I sat down with my head in my hands, my thoughts racing in all directions like a herd of frightened rabbits. Was a bunch of rabbits a herd? There was doubtless some poetic term for it, like an exaltation of larks. Why did I know that one? Some random pop song? Down down down; I began to have murderous thoughts about the gentleman of leisure who kept on singing.

'Don't you know any other tune?' I said at last, watching my hands tremble with rage, not trusting myself to look at him.

'Was I singing?' He chuckled. 'I don't even notice when I do it. My wife left me because of that, thirty years ago. Well, that and the fact that I was banging my secretary.' His smile suggested the peace of the Buddha nonetheless.

I tried to sleep, knew it would never happen and yet suddenly it was near dawn. I saw the first light of the early spring morning filter through the tiny window. My neck ached like a war wound and I put a hand up to massage it as my eyes fluttered, adjusting.

And there was Peaches.

'This is your fault, innit?' She had her fists on her hip and a snarl. 'Everything was going fine and then you got in the way.'

'If everything was fine, why were you getting a divorce?' I asked irritably.

'Part of the plan, my man, part of the plan.' She squeezed down between me and the old man on the bench. 'Getting shot wasn't.'

'You think maybe you brought it on yourself, eh?' I wasn't about to accept blame for that, especially not from her.

'You gave them opportunity!'

'But you gave them cause.' I cracked my neck. 'What's all this rabbit business? You pregnant?'

Peaches snorted. 'You're on the wrong track there, mister. Old man couldn't even get it up most nights unless he had a floor show and he had the hired help for that.'

I blinked and tried to create pictures in my head to match her words but my foggy grey cells weren't up to the job. 'So what's all this then? What's that on about? Why'd they shoot you? And blame me?'

'It's the white rabbit, see I found—' She cocked her head. 'Hang on, I have to have a word with the previous Mrs. Dockmuir. Which means a bit of a dust up first. Later, tater.'

And then there was just space and the snoring tramp and me still blinking. *Overdue at the fairy dust factory?* Or just a dream? I sniffed. I could swear I smelled her signature perfume, some fash mag slag brainchild with essence of peaches and something citrusy behind it.

Or maybe it was just a dream. I closed my eyes to find surcease of sorrow before the old man resumed droning or the drunks began retching and hoped that the fever that filled my brain might be stilled by knitting up the ravelled sleeve of care if only for a wee while. With luck I would remember nothing.

'You're sprung.'

I blinked awake again—or for the first time. The lad who beckoned looked bored and slightly irritated as I continued to blink at him, uncomprehending. I had ended up on the tile floor somehow.

'Out. You. You're sprung,' he repeated, waving me forward. I gathered myself and stood, swaying for a moment, feeling the creaks of the night's rest in the stiffness of my limbs and the muzzy cottony consistency of my brain.

But I followed him out the door and back to the release desk and signed and stepped out into the light where I was flung only to see no one I knew. Where was my counsel?

'Mr. Draygo?' A brisk young woman greeted me and shook my limp hand and beckoned me to follow her out.

'I am,' I could feel the itch behind my eyeballs and badly wanted some caffeine, some chemical calm and a collapse.

The shivers crawled up my skin. A nice soak in a tub and a little fairy dust and I would be cruising again and all this would be behind me. 'You got the paperwork? Where's Max?'

'Mr. Draygo, we need to talk about your experience with Peaches Dockmuir. I need to know—'

I stopped and stared at her. 'You're not from Clepington, Arkady & Dens, are you?'

She winced. 'No, but I need—'

'Why did you spring me?' It was too early and I was feeling too frail to deal with more complications. I just wanted to be a grateful duvet surfer.

'Let me explain,' she started looking earnest and righteous and I thought, no. *Let's nip this in the bud.*

'No, I need sleep, a bath and some chemical enhancements—at the very least caffeine—before I have anything to say to anybody especially if you aren't legal counsel. So if you want any chance of that happening take me home, and leave me alone for a few hours and then maybe we can talk. If Max Arkady says it's okay.' Something in the back of my brain suggested caution and I trust the reptile.

She pursed her lips and I noticed for the first time they were rather nice lips, but she gave a curt nod and led the way to her waiting cab and I got in, muttered the address and had fallen asleep before we pulled away from the kerb.

'We're here.'

I snapped awake and my neck objected but home looked good. Well, at least it appeared to be no shabbier than the day before and thank the Great God Pan the paps seemed to have relocated for a time. That ginger cat was nowhere to be seen, probably buggered off back home. I pounded on the door until Jinx reappeared, hugging me with a sob.

'It's not like I was dead, Jinxy,' I said, trying in vain to shuffle off his gorilla arms. 'I'm going to bed. Make sure there's some heavy weight java when I wake up, right? And her,' I looked over at my would-be rescuer. 'Whatever she wants as long as she don't get into anything.'

I stumbled down the corridor to my room and shed all my clothes. I almost wanted a bath first to scrape the muck of the cell off me, but it was too much effort. Down, down, down, the damn song in my head as I crawled under the duvet and barely had time to think of enhancing my slumber when I was out and then it was sometime later and no Peaches, no singing tramp, and no idea what time it was.

Looking at the light filtered through the curtains I would guess it wasn't much more than eleven. And probably the same day. It wasn't that bad after all. I was pleased to see Jinx had the hot water heating already and started my bath running. For a moment I thought I could smell peaches but doubtless it had been only an illusion. Was there a word for an illusion of smell? Nasal illusion? No, what's the word? I needed to recharge the nasal passages anyway and pulled open the drawer next to the bed. Ah, cornucopia.

I lay in the warm waters in bliss. Nothing as restorative as a nice hot bath. Well, a nice hot bath with chemical enhancements. And I could hear Jinx's step in the hall, doubtless bringing me some caffeine as well: good man.

Olfactory illusions, that was the word. I could smell the coffee before it arrived and it gave me a shudder of pleasurable anticipation. 'Jinxy, I have been looking forward to your magic beans.'

'I'm glad to hear it.'

My eyes popped open and I splashed helplessly. 'You can't come in here!' My voice screeched a little with unexpected alarm.

'Nothing I haven't seen before, Mr. Draygo,' she said, balancing the mug on the tray with the soap and sponge. 'We need to talk.'

'I'm having a bath here, in case you haven't noticed,' I said, trying in vain to cover up my unmentionables.

'I'll look the other way,' she said, chuckling, which did not endear her to me. Crossing over to the window, she made a show of staring out it, which was a bit difficult given the textured glass and all.

'Who are you anyway,' I asked reaching for the mug and taking a good gulp of it. Ah, bless your craggy heart Jinxy! The only thing better than his java was a cup of his java with a little kick of scotch. Almost made me feel human again which is to say, curious now. 'And why did you spring me?'

'I'm working on exposing Dockmuir and I want to know what happened before you get all cagey with legal counsel and whatnot.' She held her elbows in her hands, close against her body despite the heat of the bathroom.

'Journo, eh?' I took another gulp and let it burn its way down my throat. My brain began to wake up. 'Trying to take him down from the inside?'

She laughed, a short bark without too much humour in it. 'Yeah, I work for the rags. You know, for a washed-up has-been, addled by too many abused substances you're quick off the mark.'

'Washed up? Says who?'

'Most accounts of your brilliant career. Teaming up with Psychic Sally next?' I could hear the smirk in her voice. She seemed less tense, too, releasing the grip on her arms and leaning against the sill instead. It gave me a chance to notice the rest of her. Clad in a sensible grey suit, the tailoring didn't really enhance the fact that she had a nice form, but there wasn't much that could conceal a fact like that for long. Was she really a journo? My experience with the species generally skewed more toward pear-shaped nail chewers of the grizzled variety but maybe that was the crime beat.

'I have a booming and, might I add, legitimate business, at least when it's not being interrupted by trashy socialites who insist upon getting snuffed at my table.' I was moving back toward irritable although I had to say there was a lot to enjoy in the view before I left curious. A little more caffeine woke up the rest of my corpse and I realised I was going to need to hide my nether regions again. 'What paper are you with?'

'I have a broad portfolio. No one can afford to work for just one paper anymore. Get with the 21, Draygo.'

'I like things fine back in the nineteenth, where women were women and men were men.'

'And everyone died of cholera or tuberculosis,' she said turning around to stare me down.

A contest I lost immediately. 'Hey, turn back around. I'm still naked here.'

'I see.' She smirked. I shriveled a little.

'What's your name anyway?' I said to cover my embarrassment. 'I usually like to know the name of people who interrogate me in my bathtub.'

'Helen Saunders. I'd shake hands but—'

'Yeah, all right. Well, here's the deal. Let me finish my ablutions while you go get Jinxy to rustle us up a full English—'

'I don't want a full English.'

'Well, I do. We can talk over brekkie. I refuse to say another word until then.' I crossed my arms over my chest.

She stared at me, but slowly cracked a smile. I was right. She had nice lips. Reluctantly she walked to the door. 'Don't forget to wash behind your ears.' Laughing she closed the door behind her.

Bloody woman.

'How long have you been investigating him?' My humour had returned with the second rasher. I scooped some beans onto toast as Helen Saunders looked on with amused disgust.

'About six months. At first it was just the Panama Aircraft deal but then I stumbled across some other information that would be a lot sexier than some dodgy high finance shenanigans.'

'Let me guess, drugs?' I swallowed another generous portion of Jinxy's java plus and revelled in the warm burn.

'Have you heard of 'blue bottle'?'

'I'm guessing you don't mean the Goons,' I said, taking entirely too much pleasure in the last bite of sausage. Jinxy could pick 'em, that's for sure.

'Knock-off Viagra,' Saunders said, frowning. I could tell she was the crusader type, the righteous anger had begun its ascent and she would brook no denial of her forward charge. From which I deduced a tragedy lay not too far back in her history. 'Flooding the market lately.'

'Sounds like a global masculinity crisis.' I laughed and poured more coffee. 'This calls for new and better pin ups!'

'Amusing,' she said, her voice suggesting it wasn't. 'But that's only the tip of the iceberg—'

'So to speak.'

She made a face. 'Can you be serious for a few minutes at a time?'

'With a belly full of pork products, starch, eggs and caffeine, I can be anything you want. For a few minutes.' A little dust coursing through my veins didn't hurt either. All was right with the world now. Hard to believe I had been packed off by the filth only hours ago, cheek by jowl with the detritus of the streets. Amazing what bath and brekkie could do to restore the shape of the world. 'Lay on, Lady Macduff.'

She ignored this, too. 'There's a whole new flood of drugs on the market. Cheap so they spread; plentiful, so they're everywhere. But stories piling up, too.'

'Mysterious deaths?' I tried not to sound smug.

She nodded but tapped her finger on the table. With some discomfort, I realised it reminded me it was about the spot where Peaches' bloody head had lain not a day before. I decided to go back to eating in the kitchen. 'Deaths yes, but there's a lot more going on. I don't have enough details to be sure—'

Now my interest was piqued. 'What kind of 'details' are you talking about?'

'There's something strange about these drugs. Other effects.'

'What sort of effects?'

She shrugged. 'It's too soon to be sure…'

'But you have a theory, I can tell.' There was something unsettling in Saunders' evasion. It wasn't just the writer concealing a good lead. The possibilities freaked her a little. Something too weird to be spoken aloud—or believed?

'It sounds too naked to say 'mind control' but that's what I've been hearing.' She poured herself a shot of coffee and grimaced as she drank it. 'What the hell?'

'I like it strong.'

'And spiked. You an alky as well?'

'As well as what?' I bridled.

'A chemical brother,' she said, coolly appraising me, which annoyed me to no end. 'A dust rider, a rip snorter—how many euphemisms do you want?'

'I like a good euphemism now and then, as long as they don't get out of hand,' I said trying to conceal the bitterness. I had begun to think this woman was trouble. Of course she was; anyone on a mission would be trouble.

I had enough trouble already. 'Maybe you should be out investigating this and leave me the hell alone.'

Saunders smiled. Funny how those nice lips could look all crafty. 'Can you just tell me a couple things before you give me the bum's rush?'

'Like what?'

'Why did Peaches come to see you?'

I sipped my cup of java. 'She wanted to talk to someone deceased.'

'Don't be cagey now, Draygo.'

'I don't see why I should tell you anything at all,' I said, feeling the righteous indignation rise in my chest although maybe it was just the surfeit of pork products. 'You're just a street reporter after all and I could sell my exclusive for a good chunk of change as they say to a bigger name.'

'And be the sap who gets to be the fall guy for murder, too,' she flashed back quick as a brown fox. 'You looking forward to that?'

I laughed but I wasn't as confident as I tried to sound. 'My ex-partner's on the case. He might bear a grudge against me, but he's as honest and fair as the day is long and I know he won't pin nothing on me I don't deserve.' Not that there wasn't plenty to do just that with, come to think on it.

'Then he won't be on the case long,' Saunders said quietly. 'Dockmuir wants what he wants and he expects to get it. And clearly he wanted Peaches dead. If he's willing to knock off his wife, you think he'll cry one salty tear for you?'

I gulped down another mouthful of java to delay responding. She had a point. But could I trust her?

'Yeah, trust her, you moron,' Peaches said.

I spat out the last of the mouthful of coffee. 'What!'

'What?' Saunders said, staring at me.

I looked to my side. Fuck me, there was Peaches, large as life if no larger and smelling of her signature scent. 'What?'

'I said trust her. I can't tell you everything, but I do know that. She's got a dead woman by her side, too. Hiya!' She waved, presumably at the other woman.

'Who's the dead woman by your side?' I asked Saunders, who continued to look at me as if the top of my head had lifted off, circled the room and landed on the coffee pot.

'What?'

'Thank you for your contribution to our continuing monosyllabic conversation.'

'But—'

'More eh?' I leaned forward, enjoying her sudden confusion. 'Who's the dead woman at your side? Peaches can see her. And much as I am unamused by the doubling of the breakfast club, I want to know, too.'

Saunders stared and, with seemingly great effort, refused to look to her side. 'Describe her.'

Peaches sighed melodramatically. 'I wasn't called here to do parlour tricks.'

'Yeah, me neither,' I said, 'but somehow it's fallen to our lot, Peaches.'

'She looks like a carbon copy of this one. Must be her sister.'

Interesting. 'Can you give specifics? She's not going to believe us too easily, look at her.' Indeed Saunders appeared dead spooked but unwilling to admit it on pain of death herself. 'What's she wearing?'

'Right then, she looks like her but has little twee braids in the front of her hair which is more brown than this one's. She's wearing a Clash t-shirt and a very retro sort of black blazer with the sleeves rolled up and skinny black jeans. It's a look,' Peaches said with a dismissive shrug. 'No offense!' The latter directed at the other apparition apparently.

I relayed this to Saunders who turned several shades paler.

'Olivia,' she said with wonder, looking the wrong way.

'Other side,' said Peaches, which I repeated.

'Can she see me?'

'Of course, and hear you and what not. Smell you? I dunno. What do you say, Peaches?'

'I don't smell nothing. Are we going to get to the point here soon? I don't have all the time in the world.'

'You're giving an enigmatic view of the afterlife, Peaches,' I told her as I poured out the dregs of the pot.

'Can you shut up for a minute?' Saunders said, her voice sounding strangled as she tried to cope with the new information. 'I don't think I should believe you about all this—'

'But you do, because you have to and it's annoying, but there it is.' I swallowed the last of the java and then felt a twinge of remorse as Saunders looked like she could use a jolt as well. 'Hey, Jinx!'

'I don't understand how you could know...' She shook her head.

'Occam's razor.' I said waving the cup at Jinx as he poked his head in the door.

'What?'

'Occam's razor, the rule that—'

'I know what it is,' she broke in with evident irritation.

'Even I know what that is,' Peaches added, seating herself on the edge of the table and beginning to file her nails.

'Well, look,' I said reasonably as Jinx took off with the breakfast plates and the coffee pot. 'I met you for the first time this morning when you sprung me. I didn't even know your name until a short time ago and unless I have suddenly become a internet-savvy technical wiz in the last hour, I didn't really have time to do any research on you.'

'True enough.'

'So the simplest answer to how I could know what your dead sister might be wearing is that she's here in the room however wispily ethereal and I—or rather my compatriot Ms. Peaches Dockmuir née Weiner—can see her.'

Saunders shook her head slowly. Not denying what she'd been told, just processing it, as the kids say.

'So now can we get to the point?' Peaches said, leaving off rasping at her nails for the moment for which I was eternally grateful. I had begun to suspect that MI6 used the irritating sound as a foundation of their torture techniques.

'And which point is that, Peaches?'

'Why I was called back here, you moron.' She gave me such a look of contempt and derision that for a moment I was glad she had shuffled off the mortal coil.

'And in your estimation, other than to plague me, what is the reason you were called back here?'

'You well know! Like all the other people here, I have unfinished business. As my legal counsel liked to say, 'to whit' my soon-to-be-late husband's murder of me!' When she got wound up, Peaches managed to be quite the fireball.

'Other people?' Saunders said weakly.

'Yeah, he's been ignoring them it looks like,' Peaches said with snort.

'Not ignoring,' I protested, patting my pockets for a little boost of calm and finding a couple of Roche rumblers. I did feel that I had earned them, though another shot of that black elixir would help the blues settle nicely. Goodbye, blue Monday.

'Yeah, right. You just too busy popping them pills to listen to the last requests of the dead,' Peaches said, the scorn in her voice almost taking on physical presence.

'Oh fuck me, I hear dead people,' Saunders said, half-rising from her chair.

'It's just Peaches,' I said, my irritation overwhelming any attempt at comfort. Not that I was known for my chivalrous behaviour. 'And this room and the presence of your sister are likely raising your connection to the ether.'

'The ether...?' She sat back down, her face pinched as if it were in pain.

'Yep, it's all true, god's an astronaut, Oz is over the rainbow and your hair is your aerials. Your connection to the mystical ether. You wouldn't credit it, but the man was right.' Where was Jinxy with the java? I could murder a cuppa.

'But your hair is almost non-existent!'

I ran a hand across my stubble. 'Too right. I have more than enough antennae.' A knock and there was Jinxy with my fix. 'Bless you, my son.'

He refilled our cups and set out a third, then looked around with confusion.

'Don't worry, Jinx. Not everyone's drinking.'

'He can see them, too?' Saunders gripped her mug tightly but hadn't taken a sip.

'Sometimes. Drink, you'll feel better.'

'I doubt that.'

'Okay, you'll feel calmer.' I let the black magic burn down my red lane. 'Days like this things are a bit more busy than usual.'

'We gonna talk about my murder or what?' Peaches was getting impatient.

'All right, Peaches, let's talk about your murder. Why did you get murdered and all?'

'How the fuck am I supposed to know that? You the detective.' Her eyes blazed and I contemplated making a Hades reference but I figured being newly dead and all she might not appreciate it.

'I'm not though. I am a former detective and current struggling psychic with too few clients and too many dead folk who ought to be off enjoying the afterlife. What you need is a real detective, so go haunt yourself one.'

A knock at the door. Jinx leaned in and jerked his head toward the corridor. Now what? 'I have to see about this.'

I had just risen from my chair when my former partner burst in. 'Sit your arse down again, Jawbone. We have to talk.'

'Coffee?' I said, resigning myself to this latest twist-stroke-interloper with aplomb. Either that or the diazepam were filtering nicely through the coffee and scotch. 'I don't think anyone will mind if we use this mug,' I said looking pointedly at Peaches who huffed with annoyance.

'When we going to get to my murder?'

I held up a hand. 'This is my former partner, Langdon Coburn.'

Coburn nodded at Saunders, assuming that she had been the object of my introduction. 'Cheers.'

'Helen Saunders,' she said, though her expression continued to look a bit shell-shocked and her eyes kept drifting to the side.

'You arresting me?' What the hell: I couldn't say I minded much anymore. The quiet would do me good.

Coburn shook his head. I noticed my partner had a lot more grey hairs than he did a handful of years ago, something I hadn't noticed yesterday. And something else; there was a kind of grey pallor over his features, the coffee dark skin looking far more haggard than was the norm even for him, even after an all night watch. 'I'm off the case.'

'Told you,' Saunders said, her face grim. 'Dockmuir ordered it?'

Coburn looked at her, then at me. I shrugged and nodded. He faced Saunders again. 'Not directly, but my superior looked mighty uncomfortable and yanked me off without a word and gave it to that stiff Michaels.'

'Ah,' I frowned. Everyone knew he was one of the dirty guys. 'They can't really pin this on me, can they? I mean they can, but—are they going to?' Suddenly my blood pressure found its second wind.

Coburn shook his head. 'Can't be certain, but I don't think they're working that angle, though they might use it as an excuse anyway. They can't bury my report too easily. I got it into the right hands.'

I clapped his shoulder with genuine gratitude. 'Thanks, mate. I owe you.'

'That you do.' The words were colder than I would like, but I found myself grateful anyway. 'What do you know?'

'Peaches came here to commune with the late Mrs. Dockmuir.' I said, looking up at the queen of bling.

'What for?'

'I wanted to know what she knew about the white rabbit,' Peaches said, excited again now that the conversation had got back to her. She stood at Coburn's side, which gave my head a weird feeling of amusement.

'A white rabbit.' I figured cut to the chase. 'Mean anything to you?'

'No,' Coburn said and the way his brow furrowed I believed him.

'I kept finding it everywhere,' Peaches said with irritation.

'An actual rabbit?' Saunders cut in.

'No, well—I don't know.' Peaches sighed. 'He would mutter it in his sleep at times. And there were phone calls… then I found a memo but he yanked it away from me and told me if I wanted to live to keep my yap shut.'

'A memo, some phone calls, talking in his sleep,' I translated. Saunders and Coburn digested this while I stared at Peaches, whose face scrunched up in a crinkle of surprise.

'I'm dead. I'm really and truly dead.'

'Afraid so,' I said, shifting in my chair. She burst into tears and began wailing like a klaxon. I winced. I tried to ignore the other shiftings just behind her.

'Afraid what?' Coburn said.

'It's her again,' Saunders said with accusation. Without warning, she hopped up and ran out of the room. Coburn stared after her. I wanted to cover my ears.

'It's all your fault,' Peaches said tearfully, pummelling my arm.

'Give it a rest,' I said yanking my tender flesh away from her blows.

'What are you on about?' Coburn said, getting to his feet again and shaking his head. 'You've lost it, mate. You had something long ago, or I gave you credit for more than you had. You're wasting my time again.'

'It's not like that, you don't know,' I said desperately wishing Peaches would stop howling like that. 'You never knew, you never did.'

'See if I do anything for your sorry arse again,' Coburn mumbled, squashing his hat down on his head and walking away. He slammed the door after him.

'Could you just shut the fuck up, Peaches!' The more agitated I got the more I could hear the rumble of those behind her, too, which I was not about to allow in. Best way around this was to make like the others and exit, pursued by bear.

I rocketed out of my chair and slammed the door behind me. Grabbing my coat in the vestibule, I shouted at Jinx, 'Off for a wee while, back later.'

Then I rabbited out the door and down the street, hoping I'd left all the lost souls behind me for a time. What I really needed was a drink. A proper drink.

I walked the streets of the venerable city until a reasonable hour sidled up to me. Say what you will about this dirty old town, but its avenues greet you like old friends and offer places to wander when you want to be lost. From the posh corners to the river, it's got myriad little villages within the city, each to itself a tiny world. In better days I loved nothing more than idling along the banks of the river, mud-larking for what I might find: eighteenth century crockery or cracked mobile cases or once a heart shaped piece of red glass, smoothed by the tide, with a vein of black running through it like it was permanently broken. I carried it in my coat pocket yet. Not sure why, but you take the gifts the river offers and you make your own offerings at the turns of the wheel. Keeping balance, Auntie Vera called it. How did things get so off kilter?

I was too done over for philosophical questions. As the shadows lengthened my steps found a mind of their own and led me down the darkened streets toward a familiar light. When the world grows dark and your friends have abandoned you and all hope seems lost, the beacon you seek has a friendly face and a tap that's flowing.

Thus I found myself darkening the door of the Silver Wheel. Like most traditional pubs, it had gone through many names and many hands, though rumour had it the owners all shared the same mystical bond. Like more legends of the city, I figured it had equal parts sham and history, but I wasn't there for the tourist appeal.

'You look like you've seen a ghost,' Marinova said with a smile. If anyone else had said that, I'd have ignored it. But I knew she knew, bless her roving heart. She may have found the legacy of the pub good for business, but there was no doubt Marinova knew a thing or two about the ineffable.

'If it had just been the one ghost, I'd have been grateful.'

She laughed. Always a pleasant sound, it seemed especially so now. Without asking, Marinova grabbed a tumbler and poured a healthy measure of Lagavulin into it and a splash of water, then set it before me.

I was in her good graces for sure.

'Marry me, will ya,' I said, picking up the glass to inhale its perfume. There are few uncomplicated pleasures in life like breathing in the heady elixir of a good single malt. While I might bury myself at times in mindless hedonistic pursuits with little regard to their aesthetic pleasures, I always found time to marvel at the precise engineering that produced this bountiful alchemy. I said a prayer for the angel's share and sipped its golden gift. 'Seriously—marry me, Marinova.'

'Don't be so foolish, Draygo,' the dark beauty said with the smile that always unsettled. 'There is a woman out there for you who would be disappointed.'

'Can you see her?' I chuckled as I let the gold seep into my racing veins and slow the flood, making it flow richer somehow.

'Do you want me to look?'

A shudder went through me. I didn't want to name it. 'Ah, no. You know me, Marinova. Happy to live on in dreams of you.'

'I have dreams of my own,' Marinova said with a laugh.

'A man?'

She laughed. 'Several men. And I want to restore one of those old Edwardian palaces uptown, turn it into a swanky night club with gambling, floor shows and torch singers. Everything velvety and lush.'

'Sounds grand,' I said, her dream so vivid for a moment I could almost see it myself. I felt a stab of envy; I had no doubt the path would open before Marinova as things had a way of doing. Who was it, Emerson? What said something about the world conspiring with you once you had made a decision? 'It won't ever be so grand that I can't slip in the back for a quiet drink, will it?'

'I never forget my friends,' she said, laying a hand on my sleeve, the silver rings on her fingers flashing in the sombre murk of the bar.

'Or your enemies, eh? Only way to go,' I muttered, thinking of my own peril.

'What are the shades that hang upon you, Draygo?'

'You heard about Peaches?' How could anyone not? 'She opened a floodgate you might say.' I sighed. I could feel them all trying to get at me even now. I couldn't run forever. And I had to go home some time.

'You've been fighting this too long,' Marinova said, shaking her head as she ran a cloth in circles across the bar. The action seemed somehow soothing.

'I don't want it back,' I said as softly as I could. Though quiet, the bar was not quite empty and I didn't really want to discuss the state of my psychic doorways with just anyone. It's a private thing.

'We don't get to choose who we are, Draygo. Or what skills we receive.'

I sighed. 'Skills? Ha! Annoyance. I thought I had switched off that channel. I don't want to have to receive transmissions.'

She shrugged. 'You can refuse to accept the sun will rise each morning, too. But it doesn't change anything.'

'You're no help.'

Marinova leaned on her elbows on the bar. 'Did you come for my help?'

I fidgeted. 'I don't know.'

'Well, you didn't go to Duffy's or to the Nun & Dragon, so I assume you didn't just want a drink and a natter. So heed me. You can swim against the tide or you can use it to reach your destination. It's fatiguing and frustrating to always fight. The bee makes honey from flowers. He doesn't suck the leaves.'

'That probably means something deep,' I said, finishing my scotch. 'And I will take it under consideration.'

'Do. You have avoided the path too long.'

'I wash my own shirt. Honestly though, I haven't been up to much,' I said, laying a twenty on the counter. 'Which reminds me, you know anyone who's had some experience with fake Viagra? Not necessarily themselves, although that might be helpful, too.'

Marinova stared for a moment. 'Ah, the penny drops.'

'Not at all!' Despite myself I could feel a blush on my cheek.

She grinned. 'I know, I only meant that I have heard of the dodgy stuff. You should talk to Raphaelita, she had one just the other day. Spooked her plenty. Just watch out for Babyface. He doesn't forget.'

I grabbed my jacket. 'You're a peach, Marinova. Someday I'm going to marry you.'

'Keep that a secret,' she said, but smiled as I tipped my imaginary hat. Would that I could ever be good enough to earn her. But as she would doubtless say in her mother's wisdom, don't ask for a thing when you can't get it.

'You ever see that movie *Blue Sunshine*?' Raphaelita said as she wrung out a pair of stockings. I had pounded the pavement for an hour trying to find her place. Amazing how someone who seemed ubiquitous when you weren't looking for her could be so elusive once you were. As she hung the stockings on a miniature hanger on the line above the sink I could see that they had seams down the back like the kind women always had in old movies. It never struck me before, but Raphaelita had a whole retro vibe going.

'You ever been bit by a dead bee?' I muttered under my breath, and she turned and flashed me a smile like I'd never seen from her before.

'Walter Brennan you ain't,' she said laughing. But she seemed pleased, too.

'What's this *Blue Sunshine*?'

'It was a B picture back in the 70s. A horror film about bad LSD. People lose their hair and start killing everybody.

I used to be obsessed with it. Watched it over and over. Even had the novelisation.'

'Uh huh,' I said but wondered what the hell this had to do with my question.

Raphaelita shook her head at me. 'I thought you was a lot smarter than Babyface, but you're pretty dim, ain't ya?' She pulled the plug and let the water gurgle down the drain, then shoved me out of the way while she set up her ironing board.

'Right, I'm a little slow on the uptake today. I had to spend last night in the cooler.'

'Ah, sorry to hear that. I ain't been about today yet, haven't got the news. Whadja do? Let me guess—drunk and disorderly?' She laughed again as she spread out a shiny dress on the board.

'Hey, I have never been canned for D&D.'

'I've seen you plenty of times—'

'Yeah, but I've not been canned for it. So, tell me—what's the deal with this LSD film?'

'Just what I said; it was bad mojo and people went all ASBO after taking it. Though not right away, if I recall correctly.'

'And?' I was still mystified.

'Oh, yeah, see? The fake Viagra it's the same. Well, not the same but similar.'

I shook my head. 'People take it lose their hair and go on killing sprees? I must have missed the write up in the *Times*.'

'Dolt,' Raphaelita tested the iron with her thumb. Brave woman. 'Not that bad, but they get funny. And I ain't seen a one since they took it.'

I got a weird chill down my spine at that. 'How many of them?'

'Lessee, three I think.' She counted on her fingers. 'Robinson, Quintana and Joe Lilac, too—and he was regular.'

'They all took the fake Viagra? What happened?'

Raphaelita stared. 'What you think happened? They got wood that wouldn't quit.'

'Then how's it like *Blue Sunshine*?'

'Oh, that,' she smoothed out the folds of the bright red

dress on the ironing board. 'It was afterward. They got all weird and emotional and—well, a mite creepy, too.'

'Creepy how?'

She stared off into space for a minute, then looked back at me. 'Like they were hollowed out somehow.'

I scratched my head. 'Hollowed out?'

Raphaelita shrugged. 'I can't describe it better than that. It was like they lost something inside and were hollow. And they wandered off. None of your glad hand bonhomie. Paid up and left and wandered off like they didn't know where to go.'

'And you've not seen them since? You didn't check up on them?'

She snorted. 'I'm a sex worker, not a social secretary.'

'I was just wondering…all three of them not seen since. How regular was whatsisname?'

'Joe's a weekly. Standing appointment. Babyface was proper peeved I can tell you. Acting as if it were my fault. Like I ever fail to satisfy.'

'You mention this to anybody?'

'Other than Babyface?'

I got a bright idea. 'You got any of this fake Viagra?'

'No,' she shook her head. 'They brung it with them. You want some if I get another come along with it? You have to pay me. Or get me some of the real stuff in trade so I can swap it.'

'Deal,' I said, mind racing ahead. 'If you can find out where they got it—or if you can ask around. Anything. See what it looks like.'

'It's a little blue pill,' Raphaelita said with a shrug. 'Got a little bunny rabbit on it. Figure that's more sympathetic magic, eh?'

I could almost hear Peaches bawling in my ear. 'A rabbit? On the pill?'

'Yup. That not normal?'

'No,' I said, wondering just what it did mean, 'That's not normal at all.'

As I made my way back home I continued to wonder,

but as I got near to the homestead, the noise radiating from within made me slow my steps. The last thing I wanted was a house full of spooks. However, it looked as if I wasn't going to have much choice about that.

'Where have you been? Why don't you have a phone like a normal person?' Saunders had been wound tight as a trebuchet and exploded upon me as soon as Jinx opened the door.

'I got a phone,' I said as coolly as I could pretend to be, pointing at the Bakelite monstrosity on the miniature table in the foyer. 'It's right there.'

'What century is this?' She shook her head at me, disbelieving.

The cacophony surrounded me, Peaches loudest of all. 'I know you can hear me, Draygo! I want some answers.' Her hands on her hips and her chest thrust out, she made quite a picture of annoyed exasperation.

I shook my head. 'I'm not talking to anybody. I'm dead on my feet. I've had a lousy day and night and another day and now I'm going to go to bed and sleep a good long while and maybe, just maybe when I wake up, I will talk to some of you.'

Saunders made an 'o' with her mouth, but she shut it again and looked grim. I didn't pay her any mind. I was too busy shutting out the rest of the whining as I made my way to my own room.

I threw off my clothes, then rummaged around in my desk until a found a small bottle of red brick dust. I sprinkled the dust around bed, crawled under the covers and fell asleep without any enhancements at all.

I awoke to a strange feeling and a buzzing in my ears, which grew louder after I hopped out of bed and stepped outside of the circle. I winced. That sort of day stretched ahead of me, so before making the rounds I knew what I needed a shot of as the song went, and having no woman, I couldn't shoot her down. I did notice I was starting to get low on supplies. I would be cabbing it uptown soon. But oh, the dust felt good in my veins.

I ignored the buzzing, splashed some water on my face and wrapped myself in a dressing gown. No Jinx stirring as far as I could tell, so I'd have to perform some alchemy myself. I pattered to the kitchen. I smelled the coffee beans, but lacking ambition, put the kettle on instead. A cuppa would do me until Jinxy roused himself. I opened the breadbox and found some fragrant pumpernickel and slung a couple pieces in the toaster, while I tried to remember the last time I had made myself breakfast. I stared out the window as the kettle bubbled and the toaster got warm and wondered when things first began to go awry. That ginger cat was out in the front garden again, looking secretive as all cats do. Her life was doubtless more fulfilling than mine and probably she had someone to take care of her. A surge of fatalism washed over me. The morning light did its best to suggest that all dreams faded.

When the toast popped I slathered some good country butter on the slices while the tea steeped. The pungent aroma of the bread whetted my appetite with surprising sharpness. I sat down at the wee table with something approaching comfort. Until the door swung open and a yawning Helen Saunders came through the door.

'I'm going to start calling you 'Rust',' I threatened.

'I slept.' She shook the kettle tentatively and saw enough steam to content her. 'Cups?'

I nodded toward the shelf by her head. 'You don't look as if you slept well.'

She grabbed my Harrogate mug, stared at its fake splotch of blood, gave me a look and then dropped a tea bag into it and poured the water over it. 'Your sofa sags.'

'You should learn not to make personal remarks. And to go home on occasion.'

She ferreted through the shelf and found the sugar bowl, lifting the lid to give it a suspicious look before grabbing a couple of cubes. 'That's not very civil.'

I snorted. 'It wasn't very civil of you to play dormouse in my home without asking.'

'I wanted to talk to you… to ask you something.'

'Why is a raven like a writing desk?' I stuffed more toast in my mouth to annoy her and refuse further response.

Saunders made a face at me. 'You almost made me believe yesterday that—' She looked down at her tea as she swirled the mug. Anything but look me in the eye.

'That what?' I goaded childishly, figuring I oughtn't be the only one to suffer.

'That you could see my sister.' She did look at me then and the world of hurt in her eyes shamed me and I dropped my gaze to my own mug. Time for boosters, but my pockets were empty. I realised belatedly that I was still in my dressing robe and knotted it a little more securely.

'Auntie Vera said it was a calling and a damn fine scam, forever confusing notions of right and wrong in my head. I've always considered it an annoyance,' I said as evenly as I could manage. No use baring the soul here or anything. Nobody wanted that. 'But I see too much. And it's all real.'

Saunders remained silent for a time. 'Can you speak to her?'

I squirmed in my chair. 'Possibly.'

'Can I speak to her?'

'Always.'

Saunders winced. 'Can she speak to me?'

I sighed. 'It depends.'

'Depends on what?'

'On a lot of things. How long has she been dead? Her clothes didn't appear to be all that recent according to Peaches.'

'You couldn't see her?' Her brow furrowed.

'Apparently you are unacquainted with the luminiferous ether.' I said grandly, getting up to flick the kettle on again.

'I'm not a mark, so don't give me your patter.' Saunders frowned and moved away from me as if I might be contagious.

'It's got a lot of names and none of them right or wrong,' I said, trying to sound as reasonable as possible because I knew it would be easier that way. 'But there's a thin veil between here and there.'

'Here and there?'

'Living and dead,' I said, doing my best to stare her down. After all, this was my area of expertise.

'And you expect me to believe—'

I poured out another cup and nodded toward hers. Grudgingly, she brought her mug over for refilling. Nothing would be easy with this one. From the defiant toss of her head to the doubting brows, I could see she would baulk and question at every turn.

Time for the sideshow then.

'Bring your tea and I'll show you.' I led the way out of the kitchen. An apologetic-looking Jinx stumbled past me into the kitchen. He would make up for the missed breakfast with some fine repast at midday, no doubt.

I paused at the door to the parlour. I could hear the scrum of spirits within, all jostling for my attention. 'You have to realise something,' I told Helen, holding the door handle and feeling its minute vibrations. 'This room has been specially prepared for séances.'

Saunders raised one of those classic eyebrows at me in a now familiar gesture. 'Shaking tables and mysterious wind— and not of the 'more tea, vicar' type?'

I couldn't help a chuckle at that. This one had depths and interesting surprises that I would do well to stop considering in any way at once. 'Auntie Vera was not above the occasional commercial enhancements to the trade, but that's not what I meant.'

'What did you mean?' She looked a bit less confident now.

'It's like a megaphone to the spirit world, so hard to hear for all the shoutin'.' I braced myself for the cacophony and opened the door.

It was worse than I expected.

Having stoppered my ears for so long, there was a bit of a queue so to speak. The jangling clamour rose to a higher pitch as we stepped inside. I couldn't help wincing. I had been able to give them the cold ethereal shoulder when they came by one or two at a time, but now it was standing room you might say, so I could only see vague shapes.

I could hear though: pandemonium would not be too strong a word. A racket, a hubbub, a boisterous clamour: I ran out of words in my head as they were crowded from my thoughts by the caterwaul of demanding voices assaulted my head. Saunders stared at my evident distress, torn between natural empathy and suspicion.

I didn't care.

'In turn, you lot,' I shouted with as much menace as I could. 'Oi, Peaches!'

'What?'

I never thought I'd be so grateful to hear those brassy tones again, but her sleek dagger of a voice cut through the babble like a warm knife through butter. 'There you are, my dear.'

'Don't you "my dear me"! I've been waiting an eternity.'

Not yet you haven't, I thought but kept it to myself. 'Peaches, we need some help to get to the bottom of this matter. I don't know who killed you, but I think we might be able to do some digging.'

'You can see her?' Saunders said, clearly unable to take it in but looking nervous anyway.

'I can see her,' I said with vehemence, although I noted she was already a good bit more ethereal than she had been.

'And… others?'

'I can see some, I can sense others.'

'My sister?'

I squinted. Hard to tell. 'Peaches, is her sister still there?'

'Yeah, she's there. Now what about my murder? What do you need to know? I didn't see anything, you know that.'

Her voice sounded more sad than brassy today. Along with her increasingly transparent features, that left me worried that she wasn't holding very hard to the adjacent plane. 'You said you were conferring with the late Mrs. D. Did you find out anything more?' I tried to ignore the pinched look of pain on Saunders' face. I knew if her sister was still there all these years later, she was bound to stay for a time yet. I was a mite worried about Peaches' increasing wispiness.

'I had a good old natter with the woman. Of course we had a bit of a wrangle at first, but now we're like sisters.' She smiled and I tried to call to mind some line from a Wilde play but it was beyond the workings of my grey cells. 'Turns out she was a dancer. He do like a dancer it seems. Course it helps if she has good oral skills, if you know what I mean,' Peaches said with a snicker.

'And?'

'She got knocked off too.'

'Murdered! How?'

'Look it up. The papers—his papers—ran with the accidental overdose story. Played up the jealousy angle.'

I stared at her. 'Because you were already seeing him?'

'Yeah, of course. But he wouldn't have married me if he didn't need to cover up her murder. Poor lamb.' She appeared genuinely sympathetic to the woman with whom she'd had an otherworldly barney just recently.

'Any details about the murder we can use? She share anything tangible? Anything that wouldn't already be accounted for in the reports?' I'm not sure what I was hoping for, but there had to be something. Although what and where we could use it, I had no idea.

Peaches lounged on the edge of the table, one gold sandaled foot swinging as she pondered. 'He forced her to drink the doctored vodka and orange juice—chock full of his patented mood elevators—and get into the tub. At least she had some nice candles burning, a pretty scent to take her out. Lilac, I think. And some music.' Peaches scrunched up her face, which apparently meant she was thinking hard. 'Something about flowers. I dunno. Classical shit. Beyond me.' She shrugged.

'Well, maybe we can use that,' I said, filing it away in the back of my head. 'You had to run after her, eh? She far from here?'

Peaches looked uncomfortable all of the sudden. 'I went so far, I'm not sure where. And then I was finding it a hard row to get back here at all but I thought about how pissed off I was that he killed me and you should have warned me and I was here again. Once you get nearby, the noise alone will guide you. Kind of like my old neighbourhood,' she added with a wistful look. 'Am I going to find it hard to stay here?'

I shrugged. 'It's the natural order of things to leave.'

'I'd really like to sort things out, know he paid.' She seemed more sad than angry.

'We all want to see justice, but we don't always get it.' That was for sure. I shuddered as I sensed the small boy at my elbow, the one who haunted me. Justice eludes most of us. But maybe some people could be sorted without too much trouble—and then they could bugger off and leave me alone. 'I might better talk to a few people, just to calm things down a bit,' I told Peaches. I found it hard to hold back the hubbub much longer.

'Does that include my sister?' Saunders said. Her tone conveyed scepticism but the nerves showed through it. It must have been frustrating to hear the one-sided conversation.

I had to be truthful. 'I don't know. She's here. I just don't know if I can find her.'

'What do they want?' Saunders asked, a mixture of curiosity and discomfort in her voice.

'It varies,' I said with a shrug, working myself up to the opening. After being shut down so long, I knew it would be a wrench. 'Sometimes they want to pass messages, sometimes they want to scream, sometimes they don't even know anymore, just touch us.' I shuddered involuntarily and took another slug of java. 'They're dead. They're all messed up, as the man said.'

Saunders stared at me, looked around the room and said nothing.

I reached behind me to the sideboard, grabbed a pad of paper out of the drawer and a pencil. Kind of wish I had on more than my dressing robe; the psychological advantages of a full suit of clothing may not always be apparent, but I could yearn for them now.

I closed my eyes, leaned both hands on the table and drew a deep breath.

And then I opened my mind.

They roared in like the apocalypse, a mad swirl of voices

clamouring in every language, looking for an audience, an ear and bawling non-stop into my face. 'One at a time!' I shouted, quelling the urge to panic in my own chest. I grabbed the pad of paper and honed my thoughts on an elderly woman who seemed safe enough.

'What do you seek?'

'Tell my sister I slept with her husband,' she said with satisfaction before fading away. I dutifully wrote down, 'SLEPT WITH SISTER'S HUSBAND,' before turning to the next one. You never know, she might come back.

'What do you seek?'

An hour later the pencil and I had been worn to a nub. We had loving requests and vindictive invective, enigmatic commands and a boatload of gibberish. All delivered from the wispy beyond, in voices strident or sorrowful or desperate. It wore me down. The dead can be just as tedious as the living. The details of most people's lives are trivia to our own: the scores to settle, their lost loves, their hard-worn regrets. In the hands of all but a skilled storyteller, they become like endless stings of indifferent mosquitoes: an annoyance, an itch, no more.

But the noise around me grew less. Part of it was simply my fatigue. You could only reach across the divide for so long before you started to lose something—your patience, your strength or your mind. Pretty much in that order. My patience was wearing thin with a middle-aged geezer who droned one about his family.

'...and my son, who should have gone into the military but failed the physical requirements so he went into business but not the one my brother recommended because his mother suggested that things would go better if he took a place on the west side of town while working though he had to commute back and forth for a longer time and on the bus he ran into this guy who said he was the Buddha—'

'Is there a point to all this?' I finally broke in, the man looking vague and ethereal, as if he had worn away his own spirit with the constant sanding of irrelevant details. He gaped at me and started again with a mind-numbing assault until I was ready to scream.

I found myself grateful his recitation got interrupted even though it irked me to have a new group of people making free with my little kingdom. Jinxy burst in, barely able to alert me and Saunders before a familiar looking set of goons poured through the doorway.

'Well, well, well,' I said with a bravado I hoped covered my fatigue, 'Back to murder someone new?' Their black shirts and jeans created a similar wall of anonymity but this time I made sure to start taking notes of their individual characteristics. Unfortunately, they seemed to be hired for their indistinct exteriors. No scars, even features, a bland rainbow of flesh tones—no one too dark or too pale—vaguely masculine, but I was fairly certain that the one on the left was female.

Not sure I could point out any of them in a line up; that had to be the aim of a group like this, surely.

'Let me guess, Dockmuir wants to tell me something.' I sincerely hoped it wasn't that he wanted me dead. I kind of resigned myself to the possibility, but lately I had begun to find a new curiosity about life that made the thought somewhat melancholy. Amazing what a little mystery could do. I honestly wanted to know why he knocked off Peaches. And the rabbit thing and fake Viagra—that had begun to niggle at the back of my brain. And then there was Saunders.

Not entirely certain what I was thinking about her. But I was thinking.

One of the heavies said, 'Mr. Dockmuir wants to see you.'

'Wouldn't a phone call be simpler?' I asked, knowing it wasn't going to help in the least.

'Maybe we should call someone,' Saunders said, her voice betraying her nerves. I looked across the table and admired the jut of her chin and admired her whole classic profile. She could have rivalled Stanwyck on the screen. 'You want your representation here, don't you?'

Dockmuir's dude shook his head. 'He's a busy man and

wants to see you now.' He looked over at Saunders. 'Both of you.'

Saunders half stood, ready to resist, but I figured it would only hurt us in the end. Or they would only hurt us in the end, as well as the middle and the beginning. Besides, I had a massive migraine on its way already. 'Leave it, Saunders,' I said as gently as I could. She shot me a look of betrayal, but her features softened as she took in my state. 'We might as well know what's up with him. Jinxy, you get in touch with Max's office, tell 'em where we're bound.' I looked over at the heavies and then back at my friend. 'Just in case we don't come back.'

They took us in a plain white van, which made me chuckle a little. The svart-clad phalanx sat in a silent troop as I swallowed a couple of olly-olly-oxies to take off the edge of the long black veil.

'You think you should maybe keep your wits about you?' Saunders asked with a frown as I swallowed. 'We need all the ammunition we can get, even if it's only buckshot.'

'I'm glad to see you haven't lost your sense of humour in the midst of our travails.' I yawned. 'Wish I'd had some of Jinx's java before we were so rudely interrupted. You don't suppose they'll stop for some refuelling?' I said, eying our delivery personnel. If they heard me, they made no sign of it.

I lapsed into a doze until jarred awake by the van suddenly stopping. We must have arrived. Dockmuir's palatial grounds were on the same side of the river as every casual reader of his rags knew so well, so it couldn't have taken long to get there despite the morning traffic, though I felt especially groggy nonetheless as if I had slept longer. I suppose that was likely the effects of the oxen team carrying their relief to my noggin, but it might just as well be a side effect of opening myself up to the gibbering hordes after being shut down so long. Now I remembered one of the reasons I had done so.

You're going to guess the main reason I shut down the means of communication was something tragic, and you'd be right, but that's neither here nor there. Here being this plane and there being a short hand term for what I had actually figured out to be a shifting group of 'there'—intersecting planes of existences as far as I could tell—which wasn't far. There's all kinds of reasons to stay out of that place.

The luminiferous ether, despite the hints in the name, lacked light. I won't say all practitioners of the art fumble around in the dark; I just know that I spent an awful lot of my time bumbling like Clouseau in a blindfold. You know how atheists like to make you feel small by giving you a picture of the immenseness of the galaxy and then say, 'And you? You're smaller than a mote of dust in a distant arm of that one galaxy among billions!' If they don't poke you with a condescending finger as well, you'd be lucky.

Well, that's just the *known* world—er, worlds.

However vast the galaxies are, the luminiferous ether is vaster. Is that a word? I dunno. But trust me. You don't want to lay your hat down just anywhere in it. And if you wander in there, you want to be sure to drop some bread crumbs behind you to lead the way back.

I could have used a few breadcrumbs that morning just to lead me back to my own consciousness. The oxys and the doze left me stumbling as the crew handed us out of the van and led us into the palatial estate. Saunders had that feral look of coiled energy that somehow reminded me of a pugilist. Somehow I couldn't see her in the kit though.

'Is this the morning room?' I asked as they plunked us down on a sofa in a large bright east-facing room. Everything in the place shouted wealth in a quietly cultured voice, which led me to believe it pre-dated Peaches' arrival. Surely my dressing gown offered a *piece de resistance*. 'Does that mean there will be coffee?' My words were cheerfully ignored—by cheerful I mean that the expressions on their faces did not change as they all more or less stood at attention, waiting.

It's the habit of powerful men to make others wait. My response to the alpha dog move was to nod off once more so I could be snoring when Dockmuir arrived, although I could feel the steel tension emanating from Saunders. When one of the heavies nudged me to attention, I startled awake to see the man himself admiring his lawn from a French window. I had missed his entrance apparently.

I swear it's the normal reaction to seeing a famous person in the flesh to immediately think, 'Hey, they look just like they look like!' And he did. Everything of the polished climber from the colonies, as the old standard rag deemed him, embodied in the real thing. I could see what they meant now. It wasn't that he didn't spend a pretty penny tarting himself up nice. I'm sure that thousands went into the ensemble he sported, as well as the considered know-how of a well-seasoned Jeeves in its assembly. But it didn't matter.

Take for instance Saunders—and I was beginning to worry about the ways I was able to take her for instance. Put her in boxer's kit or a cheap suit or some kind of fancy dress costume and you would, irrespective of the outfit, say, 'There's a handsome woman.' I've known men who've come from nothing who nonetheless shined a silk suit from their given sow's ear and looked every bit the gentleman as if they were born to it—more so than some who were.

Dockmuir did not. He had the low, crafty air of street thief masquerading, trying to pull off the illusion just long enough to get away with the score. Maybe my perceptions were coloured by the knowledge that far from a heart of gold his pumping organ appeared to be made of coal, delighting in the fires of destruction whether facing a business competitor or an orphan's home slightly in arrears on the rent.

You think I'm joking? Look it up. He's the kind of man who'd buy up properties to turn orphans into the streets, then use his newspapers and media outlets to show you that they were prossy-born scroungers of the worst sort and deserved their fate due to their bad decisions' and whatnot.

Poor Peaches! You didn't stand a chance.

'I understand you claim to have spoken to my late wife,' Dockmuir said without preamble.

I didn't want to think about how quickly he'd found that out—or *how*. 'I don't suppose there's any coffee going? If we're going to have a civilised conversation, that seems like the minimum requirement.' Saunders stared at me. I liked to think she was stunned with admiration, but I suppose it's just as likely she was flabbergasted at my idiocy.

Dockmuir turned to regard me with mild surprise. Then he gestured to one of the black-clad gang and away he went to fetch some bevies. I hoped anyway. 'Are you hoping to create a controversy? Or just a mild internet sensation?' He chuckled as if he were amused. Everything about him suggested otherwise.

'Look, Peaches came to me. I didn't ask her to do so.' I yawned and pointedly looked around the room as if I were casing the joint. 'I also didn't shoot her, as you doubtless know.'

Dockmuir smiled. Now I knew how a fish in the Nile felt when he met the crocodile. 'The police must do their duty.'

'So must your employees. Did you give out a bonus for the hit?' I asked with as innocent an air as I could muster.

That wiped the smile off his face. He didn't have a ready answer for it either, I noticed. Chalk one up for me. He really had thought I'd be some kind of bargain basement psychic. Or an eejit. Probably an eejit. 'You're an ex-cop.'

'There's no secret about that,' I said evenly, my spirits raised by the sight of the heavy returning with a tea tray laden with a coffee pot, milk, sugar and mugs. And here I was expecting fine china cups. 'Or did you neglect to notice that until after you set me up?'

Dockmuir smiled. 'Paranoid characteristics. I understand you left the force under some kind of cloud, psychological wasn't it? I had assumed that was merely a kind euphemism for addiction. Common among your sort.' His colonial accent grated against the gentler words with relish and his smile got more cruel. Wonderful to see that his vicious low self lived up to every bad thing I'd heard about him.

'We had a parting of the ways that had nothing to do with my recreational activities,' I said as I reached for the mug offered by the sour looking server. 'I certainly never knocked off a wife. That takes planning.'

'No, a child, wasn't it?' That he took pleasure in the question affirmed every unkind word I'd ever heard said or seen written about him.

I tried to ignore Saunders' gaze boring into me and used all my strength to steady my hand as I brought the cup to my lips. Let the hot black elixir burn me. It wouldn't be enough to eradicate the memory—or the shadow of the boy at my elbow. 'Accidents happen.'

'Indeed,' Dockmuir agreed, 'sometimes to children, sometimes to wives.'

The fury in my chest flared bright and made me forget my singed lips. That he would dare compare their deaths! I fought to keep from jumping up and throwing the hot java in his face—not that I'd have a hope of accomplishing it with all the crew in the room. But he couldn't know the blow had hit its mark so successfully. 'Wives, hmmm. Well, as a great wit said some time ago, to lose one might be an accident. Two begins to look like carelessness. Or murder.'

His frown rewarded me. The thunderous look that accompanied it, even more so. 'You best be fucking careful about making slanderous remarks, mate.' Ah, there came the original accent in all its glory.

'Lilac?' I said, almost to myself. 'Was it lilac?'

His face turned nearly purple with rage. It took a genuine effort to get himself under control again. I suppose it was the unexpectedness of it. People often underestimate me. I don't know why. Maybe it's my easy-going demeanour, or maybe it's the shabby wardrobe. Who can say?

'Are you throwing your lot in with him?' he asked Saunders, changing tack. Clearly he didn't know how to react to me, which was just as well.

'I'm just an innocent bystander,' Saunders said with admirable aplomb. She must have decided that playing ignorant like I did would be the safest route.

'I know you've been snooping around my empire,' Dockmuir said, the latter word pronounced with a certain amount of pride and possessiveness. 'I don't like journalists.'

'That's an odd sentiment to come from the owner of several newspapers,' Saunders said with surprise.

Dockmuir shrugged. 'No, it's a perfectly natural outcome of working with the lazy bastards.' He laughed at his own joke. 'I suggest you find a more suitable target.'

Saunders shrugged. A woman of few words, most of them scathing. And a nice profile. Damn her anyway. 'I just follow the story.'

'There's no story here,' Dockmuir said, smiling as if we were all friends again. 'I'm willing to overlook your interference and slander—for now,' he added, the smile fading. 'Call me sentimental.'

'Only the best for Peaches,' I said absently, sucking back more of the brew. Damn fine brew it was, too.

'I bear you no malice.'

'That's what the mongoose said to the cobra.'

Dockmuir looked from me to Saunders and back again. 'Do we have an understanding?'

Saunders remained silent, so I said, 'I'm a little slow. What am I supposed to have understood? Could you spell it out? I promise to take notes this time.'

'Leave off,' Dockmuir said. 'I don't want things to have to get ugly.'

'Never that,' I said as if promising.

'Do you always have to have the last word?' Dockmuir said with a strained smile.

'No.'

'Are you sure?'

'Absolutely.' I sipped the last of my coffee. I figured there wouldn't be any more on offer that morning. Sure enough, the man of the people nodded to the heavies who escorted us back to the van and we were off once more.

'Did you have to be such a berk?' Saunders said, practically tutting.

'I don't know what you mean,' I said smiling seraphically. The oxys and the caffeine mixed together to bring me an angelic peace that would last at least another fifteen minutes by my reckoning. 'I tried to be cooperative.'

She snorted at that. Actually snorted. The woman had

quite the arsenal of feminine wiles. 'I can only imagine what passive resistance looks like.'

'I taught Gandhi all he knew.' I said, sizing up the heavies in hopes that they were not planning a little recreational GBH on us. At the moment I didn't much care, but I would once the dancing began. 'People come from miles around to ask for my advice on getting along with their neighbours and intractable enemies. They call me The Negotiator.'

'Who does?'

'Well, no one yet,' I admitted. 'But any day now.'

In a wee while, unexpectedly, the van stopped in a taxi lane in Trafalgar Square. I squinted at the gaudy window of the Texas Embassy and wondered what fresh hell this portended. 'You two. Out,' the adjacent heavy said, his accent betraying a Mancunian home.

'Here?' I said, uncomprehending. The noise of the tourist mecca enveloped us through the open door. 'Surely not.'

To remove any doubt, we were unceremoniously shoved through the door onto the pavement. Saunders landed on her feet, ever the cat, but I dropped to the ground like a jettisoned sack of potatoes. The door slammed shut and the van pulled away at once.

'Thank you for a lovely time,' I mumbled from the ground. 'We must do it again next week.'

'Get up,' Saunders said crossly, grabbing me by the arm with more roughness than one likes to have at moments like that.

'Ow.' I stood blinking in the unaccustomed morning light. Late morning; I squinted up at the tower of St. Martin in the Fields and smiled. 'This way,' I said, grabbing Saunders' arm, turnabout being fair play and all.

'Where are we going?'

'Need you ask?' I said.

Although it has been gobbled up by the inexorable behemoth that is the big W, The Moon on The Mall remains a comfortable pub with a warm interior only occasionally marred by tourists who've wandered off the square at peak hours. The pleasant surprise of a good guest ale cannot be overlooked.

'Isn't it a bit early yet?' Saunders said doubtfully, but didn't drag her feet too much.

'What'll you have?'

'Coffee.' She made the word a rebuke.

I shook my head. 'It's not going to compare to the high class sludge we got at the big man's palace. You're bound to be disappointed.'

She just stared at me, so I took off to the bar to order. 'A fine morning it is,' I said cheerily to the young woman pulling pints. She seemed not to notice my attire.

'You're not working,' she pointed out, her Eastern European pronunciation lilting the phrase nicely. 'Or you might feel differently about it.'

'Ah, but I am. I just have more flexible locations and duties,' I said with a sage nod. I choose a likely looking porter and ordered Saunders' coffee.

'You are a fortunate man,' the youngster said as she returned my change. I wondered about that as I balanced the drinks back to the table. Maybe it was a sign that things were looking up. Either that or the oxys were still performing their magic.

'So what do you think that cat and mouse was all about?' Saunders said as I sipped the porter. It was a touch too sweet but had a nice finish, almost chocolatey. I noticed that she barely touched her coffee. I expect it was wretched. Life is too short to drink bad brew.

'Are you sure you don't want a cuppa instead? The tea is at least drinkable.' She shook her head, looking a bit dazed. I suppose she wasn't accustomed to this sort of thing. Meaning being rustled out to a billionaire's palatial town home for a dressing down in a dressing gown before elevenses. 'He wanted to size us up.'

'Think so?'

'Next time he sets the heavies on me.' I took another mouthful of the porter. Definitely growing on me. Needed a little dust, but my pockets were empty. 'I don't think he considers you a threat at all,' I said to be reassuring though I wasn't convinced of the truth of my own words. 'He's accustomed to getting his way. Slack that.'

Saunders stared at me with a look that seemed suspiciously speculative. 'What is your damage?'

I gave her a look of exaggerated surprise. 'I didn't know you were down with the kid's lingo.'

'Seriously, what damaged you? I heard what Dockmuir said about a kid—'

'Well, you can just forget that,' I said, doing my best to keep the demons on lock down. 'Nothing you want to know about.' Chance would be a fine thing, eh? A reporter put off the trail by that kind of blunt refusal.

She was wise enough to try a different tack. 'Do you think you and Peaches can find enough information to hang him on his first wife's death?'

I found I could smell Peaches' fragrance ever so slightly, but clamped my mind down tightly against it. 'I notice you're not denying the late Mrs' story anymore.'

Saunders grimaced. 'I noticed he reacted to your information about the scene. He wasn't prepared for that.'

'Underestimated me, to his chagrin, of course.' I smiled seraphically, again. I was almost feeling as light as a seraph. That couldn't last, but I would enjoy it while I could. 'And pooh-poohed my abilities. Tut!'

'There's every reason to think you're a nutter and a liar,' Saunders said without apparent rancour. I blamed the bad coffee.

'Ah, but I have access to information that he considered private and personal—and unknown. If we can chip away at enough to unsettle him—'

'You can get him locked up?'

I shrugged. 'More likely he'll have us bumped off, too.'

'Now it's 'us' again.'

I drank more porter to avoid answering. I didn't really know what to do with this woman. But I didn't find myself all that eager to get rid of her.

'Why can you find the dead?' Saunders asked, her voice quiet. 'Shouldn't they have, you know, moved on?'

I stared off into space for a minute. There was never an easy way to make people understand this. 'A wise man once said that the dead have their highways. They also have their cul-de-sacs. When they get stuck in those little places, it's easy to communicate, especially if they're somewhat adjacent to here.'

'And if they're on the highway?'

I shrugged. 'Sometimes you can call them back.'

'If the need is urgent?'

'If the connection is strong.'

She seemed to digest this. 'Connection between you and the, er, deceased?'

'Not necessarily, but between them and the person who wants to talk to them. Hate or love tend to be the best connections. No surprise.'

The pain on Saunders' face made me want to change the subject. I know she wanted to ask about her sister, but I didn't know how much I would be able to tell her. Unless she wanted to dive in herself.

You might think that anybody who could make the link would. Saunders was smarter than that. See, you start playing with the veil and all kinds of things start to pass back and forth where they weren't meant to be. It's just common sense.

We all know how common common sense is.

Saunders remained silent, staring off into the distance. I suspected she was thinking about her sister so I let her and enjoyed my pint while considering the one after it, until I remembered my empty pockets and instead longed for my drawer of delights, which made me decide to head home.

'When can I talk to my sister,' Saunders said quietly, without warning.

'Whenever you like,' I said, wincing a little because it might not be true. 'Probably.'

'Probably.' Not a question so much as a reminder.

'We might need intermediaries,' I offered. 'And she may not actually speak.'

Saunders looked at me, gauging my truth I suspected. 'No?'

I shrugged and downed the last of my porter. 'We won't know until we try. C'mon.' I led her out the door to the bus stop.

One of the chief appeals of the Moon was its placement on two of the most convenient bus lines. I knew Saunders wouldn't be keen to float the conversation among others and she kept quiet while waiting, turning over thoughts of her own, I guessed. When the 59 arrived I hopped up to the top and picked up a discarded paper to read. Saunders stared out the window the whole way, or at least she did when I sneaked a glance her way.

I didn't know if she would want to try to contact her sister right away when we got back, but I was already beginning to think of excuses why we couldn't. I'm not sure why, but I tend to follow my gut reactions when I am in my right mind and I seemed to be then—something I would amend as soon as I could. I wanted to ask her how long she was planning to hang around, but, 'Are you ever going home?' seemed rude even to me.

Worse, I wasn't sure how I wanted her to answer that. And that uncertainty made me more uncomfortable than before.

I pretended to be absorbed in my borrowed rag all the way back to the house. Mostly because I didn't know what to say; it's good to have a barrier between you and something difficult. Saunders did notice, however.

'I didn't know you were such a big fan,' she said, looking at the garish photo of a ubiquitous pop star.

'I have always had a lively interest in her career,' I muttered. 'Let's hope Jinxy is about.' I rang the bell. While trying to look nonchalant I noticed the ginger cat sitting by the hedges that were badly in need of a trim. Whose cat was she anyway and why was she always hanging about?

'You don't have keys to your own house?'

'It's my Auntie Vera's house.'

'I thought she was dead—' Saunders stopped herself and regarded me with an odd look. 'Is she still hanging about?'

I shrugged. 'Not that I've seen.'

'Then why no keys?'

I laughed. 'Because I'm always losing them.'

'What if Jinx is out?'

'I go to the pub.' Then the door opened and a harried looking Jinx met us, nodding his head toward the foyer, where an unfamiliar figure awaited us.

Was I never to have any peace?

The figure came forward. Another woman and I steeled myself for annoyance, then did a double take. 'Raphaelita?'

'Hey, Draygo,' she drawled. 'I was about to give up and go.'

'Sorry, didn't know anyone was waiting,' I shook her hand and marvelled at her appearance. 'I've never seen you in your civilian clothes.'

Raphaelita grinned and pulled at the well-worn Arsenal shirt. 'I don't usually wear it outside, but it's my day off. I can lounge.'

'Not that I'm less than filled with delight to see you, Raph, but I suppose there's a reason you dropped by.'

She grinned and took something out of her pocket. 'Ta-dah!'

In her palm lay a small blue pill. I leaned in to take a closer look. Sure enough, the small rabbit logo graced its side. 'Aces!'

Raphaelita's palm closed. 'What'll you give me?'

'Twenty?'

She shot me a look that said 'get real'. 'Barely covers cab fare, Draygo.'

I sighed. 'Fifty.'

Her palm opened again. I took the pill and shuffled through my pockets, pulling out various bills until I made up the full amount, stuffing the crumpled notes into her hand. 'Thanks.'

'A pleasure as always. Afternoon,' she said to Saunders on the way out, giving her the up and down quite openly then cocking an eyebrow at me with a nod.

I could feel my neck flush. 'Be seeing you.'

Jinx stared after her then finally closed the door.

'We have anybody else coming by unexpectedly?' He shook his head and jerked a thumb over his shoulder. 'Lunch would be most appreciated, thanks.'

I looked at the little blue pill in my palm. The rabbit looked like it was running. I suppose if it chucked back a few of these it would be scrambling to find the nearest doe.

'I didn't realise you suffered from an embarrassing male complaint,' Saunders said, her voice dripping with acid.

'It's not the real thing, it's a fake.'

'More fool you,' Saunders said, but looked questioningly at me.

'See this symbol on it.' I held it up.

'Rabbit,' she said then her eyes widened. 'Rabbit!'

'Indeed. Raphaelita has had some weird experiences with men who've taken these rabbit pills and not been the same since.'

'Not been the same?'

I nodded. 'The word she used was 'hollowed out'.'

'That's two words.'

'Ever the pedant.' I snorted. 'I take it she meant they offered something that wasn't just erectile function but had an ulterior purpose.'

'Like…?'

What to say? I had a theory floating in the back of my head. Must be that weird *Blue Sunshine* nonsense Raphaelita went on about, but the idea had sparked and it was growing. 'Some kind of suggestibility.'

'You mean mind control?' Saunders seemed to entertain the idea, which gave me a little confidence.

'I think that's one of the possible aims. Wouldn't be too outlandish with someone like Dockmuir behind it.'

'But mind control?'

'Suggestibility,' I said, warming to the topic. 'Making your sales better, getting more docile consumers. I could see it.'

'I suppose…' She didn't appear to be convinced however. 'What's in it?'

'Only one way to find out.'

Saunders look properly horrified. 'You're not going to—'

I laughed harder than I had in many a long day. 'I'm taking it to a lab. Jesus, Saunders, you are a weird woman. Or were you getting your hopes up. Hopes up! Get it?'

'Shut up and let's have lunch.'

'So what do you think it is?' I asked, trying inexpertly to mask my eagerness.

She stared at me. 'Don't be a ballbag. I'm supposed to tell by turning my laser vision on it? Oh, wait, maybe you wanted me to use my superhuman sense of smell? Let me change in the phone box over here first.'

Maude van de Peer was the best in the business—the business being chemical analysis—so she didn't have to play nice with anyone. I think she enjoyed taking the piss out of me in particular, but maybe that was because she liked me. Not enough to introduce me to her fellow Swiss friend and (I suspected) MI6 agent who had been dropping off a sample the same day as me once—a gorgeous and lethal woman with honey coloured hair and amber eyes, who looked like she could kill an entire squadron of career spooks without breaking a sweat and still be ready for a stroll down the red carpet. They were chums, clearly. But no, not enough to do that.

Huh. Maybe she didn't like me at all.

'Yeah right, I get you.' I frowned. 'I just wondered if you might know what would sort of provoked those reactions.'

'What did your friend say? 'Hollowed out'? Let me consult Merck's for that side effect.'

I winced. 'I think it might be related to mind control.'

'I must raise an army of zombies to do my bidding,' she said in a Karloff voice, raising her arms to demonstrate the typical zombie shamble.

'That was Lugosi,' I said with a touch of triumph in my voice.

'Oh, fuck yeah. You're right.' Slightly chastened, she looked at the little blue pill again. 'They've taken pains to make it look legit to the casual observer.'

'Have you seen any other knock-offs with the rabbit logo?'

Van de Peer turned it over in her palm. 'No, can't say that

I have, but we get a shed load of this bollocks through here. I can check any samples in transit. Is it just the fake V? Or are they covering all the bases?'

'We don't know,' Saunders put in, obviously wanting to be part of the conversation. She had watched our sparring with amusement. 'But we do think there might be some kind of behaviour modification at work, trying out formulas to make people more pliable. Just a theory.'

'Fluoride in the water, eh?' Van de Peer nodded. 'Could be.'

'Wazzat?' I asked, as the two of them seemed to know what it was they were talking about.

'Back in the mid-twentieth century, it was a conspiracy theory thing,' Saunders explained. 'Mostly in America.'

'Though there were fluoridation brouhahas in Ireland and the Netherlands, too,' Van de Peer added. 'The same sort of blather.'

'Mind control?'

'Or poison,' Saunders said. 'You know, the communists are coming to get you and they will stoop at nothing. Like poison in your water.'

'Good excuse to drink beer.' They didn't laugh. I let the pause drag on. 'So, like the numpties who refuse vaccinations because they think they 'cause' autism?'

'I love the internet,' Saunders said dryly.

'Never have so many believed so much ballbaggery on so little evidence,' Van de Peer agreed.

'You like that term.'

'It's a good term. Suitable for any occasion,' she added in a rather good Hepburn voice.

We left her with promises to ring Saunders' mobile if she turned up anything conclusive. 'It would be better if I had more than one fucking pill to work with. Get it? Fucking pill! Viagra! I'm a genius.'

'She's good though,' Saunders said as a kind of question as we stepped outside.

'Best there is. That's why she gets to take the piss out of everyone.'

'So what's next?'

I stared at her. 'Pub?'

'I think I'll head to the BL. I want to do some digging in the newspapers for any mention of fake Viagra or some such kind of thing. Any uptick in drug weirdness. Anything suspicious.' She looked at me with what was doubtless meant to be a significant glance.

'Yeah, pub.' I mostly said it to see her blood pressure rise, which it did. 'Just joking. I have a long line of folks waiting to give me messages.' *Although a stop by the pub wouldn't be a bad idea*, I promised myself.

'I guess...' Saunders looked away and then back again. I couldn't tell if she was angry or what. 'Well, if I find anything. Or if you find anything...'

'What?'

She made a sound of annoyance. If I had to describe it accurately, I'd say it was somewhere between a harrumph and a squeak. 'You have my number.'

'Do I?' I rifled through my pockets. 'Did you give it to me?'

'I gave you my card!'

'I know, it's here somewhere. Or Jinx has it.' I clung to that thought. 'Yeah, I think Jinx has it.'

She stared at me a moment, then reached in her own pocket to extract another card. 'Put it in your hat band.' Then she walked off swiftly.

I stared at her departing figure, squelching the urge to shout, 'But I don't have a hat!' in her wake. A peculiar creature that one.

Without consulting my A to Z, I had the feeling that I might be able to find a pub nearby. Sure enough, the woodsy door frame of a public house beckoned from around the corner. A number of lab coats spoke of its geography in the hospital region, but they had a nice selection of ales on display, so I asked the Polish lad behind the bar to pour me a fine one, promising myself I'd only have two before heading home.

There's something relaxing about being in a pub.

Everyone's there for the same reasons, more or less: chat and guzzling. If you only wanted one or the other, you'd go somewhere else. I suppose there might be a third reason of wanting to avoid going home—who? me?—but for the most part it was a positive thing you sought out. While the familiarity of the local has its pride of place, where change of any kind is frowned upon, there's a lot to be said for wandering into a pub you've never seen before and might never see again. Maybe it's my gypsy blood. Maybe it's the need to be free of expectations and disappointments. The blank slate: that would make a good name for a pub.

I had ordered a pint of Scottish ale and found it to have a good, sharp taste with a little bit of a sweet finish. I noticed that at the big table in the middle of the room they were clinking glasses with the ostentatiousness of people unaccustomed to raucous celebration. Their white coats presumably marked them as part of the hospital and laboratories around here. An idea hatched in my head without my wanting it to do so.

I took my pint in hand and walked over. 'You lot find the cure for cancer today?' They turned to me, pleasant smiles on their faces, an openness I was unaccustomed to seeing.

'Not quite,' an older man said, grinning. 'But we might be one step closer!' They all clinked glasses again. *Look at that, saviours of the world and nice people, too.* The bunch of them tried to explain to me what it is they had done, but quickly lost me in the technical terminology. I hoped it was technical anyway, because I was completely befuddled.

'I'll take your word for it,' I finally said as they beckoned me to join them. 'I didn't follow most of that explanation. I'm sure it was very important though,' I added as I sipped my brew.

The sole women among the white coats laughed. 'You sound like my husband.'

A thin young man with a long Thai name on his badge snorted. 'It's not really that difficult as long as you know a little computational chemistry and the patterns of linear regression—'

'Which I can assure you I do not. I'm ready to run now.'

That proved a hit and they all laughed. The group went on excitedly for a time and I strained to follow the bouncing ball of the conversation but it proved to be a struggle indeed. 'Wait. What's that? You came up with this fancy new drug but you lot don't actually have the patent?'

The woman gave me a pitying look. 'That's the way it works in the industry. On the plus side, there's no way any of us on our own could afford to fund a laboratory as state-of-the-art as this one, or stock it with the best and the brightest.' She clapped the Thai guy on the shoulder, but he didn't seem to realise the compliment.

'The drug company is going to make a bajillion from this,' he said, shaking his head at the unfairness of it all.

The white haired older guy chuckled. 'True enough, but they're also going to have to fund all the trials and the eventual lawsuits, too.'

'Lawsuits?' This was a side of drug development that had never occurred to me.

The woman nodded. Her name tag read *Johnson*. 'There will be lawsuits for side effects, lawsuits from other pharma companies, lawsuits from other labs who will claim they got there first, and the list goes on.'

'Yeah,' said the Thai guy, 'But they'll corner the market, charge hideously high prices and cash in beyond all imagination. And we'll just get our bonuses—if we're lucky.'

That seemed to suck a bit of the joy out of the room. Nice kid: he doubtless had a bright future ahead of him, which he would never enjoy. I tried to kick the ball back into play. 'I suppose the lure of riches motivates some people to become freelancers.'

'Well, it's a rare person who can afford to fund a major research lab without being tied to one of the pharma corps,' Johnson said.

The older guy eyed me. 'You don't mean independent labs, do you? You mean crime.'

'I'm just wondering,' I said shrugging. 'Somebody has to

know something to make all the illegals, right? People with some training.'

'And no morals,' Thai guy said. 'The atrocities they perpetuate are too horrible to contemplate, the lives ruined, the innocents killed.'

His ferocity surprised me, as I had pegged him as a likely candidate for going freelance. 'There's so many risks involved, but there seem to always be new drugs on the street.'

'Are they really different?' Johnson asked. 'Or are they just giving them new names?'

'What are you drinking?' The older guy asked me before he went up to order us another round.

'How hard is it to come up with new drugs?' I found myself genuinely curious.

'Effective drugs,' Johnson said, 'they take a bit of doing. If you just want to make some minor changes, it's a piece of piss.'

'There are two basic types of drug design,' the Thai guy said, 'Ligands or structures. Depending on whether you want to employ crystallography or spectroscopy to determine the target structure...'

'In my head your words have become the Banana Splits theme song,' I told him. He stared at me uncomprehendingly. 'Yeah, kind of like that look. Before your time, mate.'

Johnson laughed. 'Two basic models: you look at how the molecules bind together and try to find ways to make them do so more efficiently, or for a different effect I suppose. The other is to tinker with the structure of a drug and see if you can make it work more efficiently within the target organism.'

Returning with the drinks, the older guy added, 'You really have to combine the two to know whether your drug will succeed.'

'What if you wanted to hide one drug inside another?' I asked.

'Hide it?'

'Well,' I hemmed, trying to figure out what I was asking. 'If you wanted to combine two drugs, but not let people know—at first anyway—that the second one was there, too?'

They all stared at me like a herd of gazelles scenting a lioness. 'You're talking about something highly unethical,' Johnson said at last, giving me a look I hadn't seen since Auntie Vera died.

Criminy, they think I—'What I'm saying is I may have uncovered an attempt to do just that. I just dropped off an example with my mate,' and explained the whole business. Of course they knew van de Peer.

Their faces became even more grim. 'That's something that would take a lot of investment and time. And a complete lack of ethics,' the white haired guy said, almost growling.

'Do drug companies have ethics?' I asked, genuinely curious though I could hear 'Rowche Rumble' looping in my head.

They were all silent for a moment, not exactly uncomfortable, but sort of sad. Johnson finally said, 'Not necessarily the companies. Most of the people who work for them do. They believe in the good they can do.'

'No one is free of the taint of commerce,' the Thai guy said.

'We have to balance research advances against ruthless capitalist overlords,' the old guy said.

'Hey, I didn't mean anything by it. We're all sinners as my Auntie Vera would say,' I tried to reassure them. 'I hear even Gandhi took a lolly from a wee babe once.'

'We've saved lots of lives,' Johnson said, her chin jutting out just slightly. 'Though we've helped make some awful men awfully wealthy, too. It's a trade off.'

'The good will live on,' I pointed out. 'The people you saved will live on.'

The old guy snorted. 'What was it Shakespeare said? The evil that men do lives on after them, but the good is usually buried with their bones.'

'Yeah, but he also said, 'Eat drink and be merry for tomorrow we die.''

'I think that's Marlowe,' the Thai guy said, frowning with concentration.

'But he did say, 'Strive mightily, but eat and drink as

friends." Johnson said with a firmness of purpose as she rose. 'Another round?'

By the time I staggered out of there we were well-sworn as friends. I wandered down the streets of the old city newly born. New friendships baptise us afresh. Surely the Bard said that or something like it. They give us new eyes and suddenly the dirty old town sparkles with hidden lights. Either that or it was the last shake of fairy dust that winged my feet as I stumbled homeward, stopping off for a curry on the way though it was early yet.

'Jinxy my man,' I said expansively as he let me in the door, 'We live in a mighty city with the whole of a grand race of fairy folk in its arms.'

'Where you been?' Peaches tapped her foot with arms crossed and a glare that could drop a rhino at fifty paces.

I winced. That she was the last thing I had expected meant that I had become rather foolish to imagine that she would be gone or that my dealings with her were done. 'Give a man a night off, Peaches. I'm in no mind to delve into the veil with a belly full of fine ale soon to be joined by this most exquisite curry dinner I have here.'

'You saw him, right? Did you let him know we're on to him?' She followed me into the kitchen, jabbing away with her insubstantial digits.

'I dropped hints,' I said, opening the Rogan Josh and inhaling its aroma with pleasure. Jinx handed me a plate and some silverware and then sat down opposite, glad to see that I had enough for both of us. We dug in with relish. I tore off some paratha and scooped up some of the tomatoey sauce and stuffed it in my mouth. It seemed like ages since I'd eaten anything.

'Hints!' I could feel the force of her impatience with me. 'I want this man to suffer! I want him to pay! I want him dead so I can kick his arse myself.'

'Well, I don't want to be locked up for making that happen,' I said as reasonably as I could manage. 'So you're going to have to show some patience.'

'Patience!'

'It's not as if you have any pressing matters,' I said tactlessly but I wanted to enjoy my meal in peace. That, perhaps, was not the way to achieve peace.

'I'm going to make your every waking moment a living hell if you don't shape up and do something about this.' Peaches seethed with fury. Worse her sparking anger began to draw a crowd again. They had drifted while I was out, but having returned they once more sought my light.

I should have stayed at the pub. How I wish I had a jingling gold coin for every time that thought has visited me.

'Look, Peaches—and the rest of you lot,' I added, glancing around. 'I want to eat my curry in peace. If I feel up to it, I will try to do more transcribing of messages. But I'll remind you, Peaches,' I pointed a fork in her direction. 'You need me. Don't piss me off.'

Jinx got up and put the kettle on. I nodded. Despite what everyone always thought about him, Jinxy was on the mark almost always in the important things.

I was happy to see the spooks gave me a little more elbow room for a time, though Peaches wouldn't leave, but sat silent and glaring from another chair. Refusing to speak, her face curled up in a snarl, she nonetheless exhibited a certain amount of patience while I ate, savouring every bite.

Jinx rolled himself an oversised spliff, which suggested he thought it was a grand meal, too. 'All right, Jinxy?' I said and he nodded as we sipped our tea. It was as close to domestic as things got here.

I had just about begun to think about carrying through with my promise to open up the brain pan a little when I heard the phone ring out in the foyer. I took my time getting to the shrill summons, so it had to be someone who knew I didn't carry a phone in my pocket. When at last I retrieved the handset, the feeling of slight annoyance I usually felt at its ring was absent, as I had slipped into a mindset sufficiently mellow as to hold a certain amount of magnanimity for the human race as a whole. Surely it rang through my dulcet tones as I said, 'Hello.'

'Oi, Draygo,' my interlocutor responded rather more

harshly than was strictly necessary. 'I've got more of those pills for you.'

'Ah, Raphaelita, so lovely to hear from you.'

'Do you want them?'

'Er, sure, sure. Why don't you drop them by?' I looked at my watch but the time didn't really mean much of anything to me. It wasn't as if I kept office hours.

'Ah well, I'd rather not come inside, if it's all the same to you,' she said, her voice taking on a certain hostility in its harshness now.

'What?'

'You heard. I don't want to come in there.'

I shook my head. 'Why? What's wrong? Hey, you're not objecting to the spooks are you? It's not their fault they're dead.' I had a feeling my head wasn't as sharp as it should be. Why would she develop a sudden sensitivity to the spectres? Had word begun to get around? Who would be yapping? It sure wasn't Jinx. I doubted it was Saunders either. Did she even have any friends? Where did she go when she left here? The British Library must be closed by now. 'What?'

'I said, come out here.'

'Where?' I shook my head to try to clear it.

'Out here, this park, like. In the middle of the square.' We were in a fortunate corner of the city with a little private garden in the middle of our square. Not the sort of thing people generally associated with south London. Most of the folks around here enjoyed it almost daily and did their bit to keep it looking nice.

'Ah.' I hung up and opened the front door, squinting into the darkness. I saw a shape that looked like Raphaelita, more or less, standing by the gate to the garden in the square.

'Hello beautiful,' I sang out as I crossed the quiet street. 'How's tricks, so to speak? What have you got for me?'

Raphaelita looked quickly from side to side. 'Don't you have a key to this thing?'

'What? No.' I shook my head. 'Auntie Vera had it some-where, but she passed on without giving me that secret. Hey, that's something I should ask her, eh?' It might seem amazing but that was the first time I had considered doing my own parley with the other side. I didn't have much truck with them if I could help it.

'Whatever,' Raphaelita said, looking past me as if to gauge the traffic coming through the square, which was pretty much nil this time of night. 'Didn't know you lived so posh.'

I snorted. 'Yeah, I think the PM has bought a house around the corner, really putting Stockwell on the map.'

'Hey, I didn't mean nothing,' she said vague, looking over her shoulder now. 'Just you know, not what I expected. But quiet.'

'Yeah, quiet. The riots stay away on the other side of Clapham Road. Better access to pubs.'

'Yeah,' she agreed, but I didn't get the feeling she was listening.

A little too late on the uptake, I finally looked in the same direction she had cocked a glance and stood there mouth agape as I saw a couple of Babyface's heavies heading my way with their marching shoes on. I turned to give Raphaelita a piece of my mind but she had already hightailed it down the street the other way, her heels clicking loudly in the silence. The brutes had their Docs on. Nice thing about those shoes: wear like iron, go with everything, don't make a noise until they kick you in the face.

Actually, they don't make a noise even then, but you do.

I made plenty of noise, but my neighbours being the curtain-twitching kind of folks didn't come out to aid their fellow man. I tried to ask for an explanation from my attackers, not that it would have made much of a difference I suppose, but you know—a man gets curious when his face is full of shoe leather.

Something snapped that might have been a rib, but mostly I was protected by the flab of a largely sedentary life with ample application of ale and lager. The ales I had consumed in the afternoon helped the curry splash about in my insides and threaten a return engagement with my mouth, but I tried to fight it back down as I curled up to vainly hide from the kicks and blows coming my way.

When I had been sufficiently tenderised, my brain screaming pain and my body offering a gibbering prayer for surcease of sorrow, the two of them stood breathing slightly heavily. Apparently it takes a lot of effort to beat someone senseless or in the vicinity of senseless, near enough to see it with a squint. *I hope you have stiff muscles in the morning*, I wished as I tried not to vomit, but wisely kept my thoughts to myself.

'Stay out of things what aren't your business,' one of them sneered before slapping his mate on the back and turning to leave. They started singing a footie song as they sauntered off. *Chelsea supporters, wouldn't you know it?*

As I lay dying, or what I figured would be relieved by dying, I had a think. *Would Babyface consider this the end of things? Was he really so mad that I didn't pay to talk to Raphaelita? Or did he just not like me asking questions? Was it my imagination, or was the pavement getting softer?*

An angel awoke me. No, wait. Greta Garbo in her shortie nightie. No, it wasn't after all. It was Saunders. My confusion was entirely understandable in light of the circumstances.

'I thought you were dead,' she said, kneeling down beside me, looking as if she'd dropped a soup bowl from her second best china set.

'I am,' I wheezed. 'Get Jinx.'

'I can help you,' she said, a hint of crossness creeping into her voice.

'Can you carry me? He can.'

She gaped at me. 'Should I call an ambulance?'

I made a mental inventory of all the painful new locations currently screeching. With an effort I pressed on my suspect rib, drawing in a sharp hiss of breath involuntarily. 'I don't think it's bad enough for that. Just get Jinx, please.'

It must have been the 'please' that put wings on her steps. My head made a second inventory, considering what I had to relieve the opera of shrieking agony that filled my flesh. It provided the one bright light. Well, there was the streetlight haloed above me, I noted. A woman in what I took to be Regency clothes leaned over me, her head ringed by the streetlight, which also shone through her face.

'Are you injured? Should I call someone for you?'

I was touched by her concern. 'They're sending someone, I think, but thank you.'

She faded away. I didn't know if she was a ghost or a fever dream. I opened my eyes again to see that damn ginger cat who opened its mouth but instead of a meow said something in French. I closed my eyes, wondering if I dared open them again. When at last I did, I was eternally grateful to see Jinxy galumphing over before any more peculiarities appeared.

He picked me up with a gentleness no one would suspect him capable of—at least no one who had seen him pummelling opponents a decade ago—then carried me inside where Saunders waited, looking admirably concerned. 'Do you need anything?'

'Water.'

Jinx set me on my bed and I started to loosen my tie while he helped get my shoes off. Saunders set the glass of water on my nightstand and stood awkwardly by. 'I think I can cope,' I said trying to smile, though my cheek felt immobile.

'You want a cloth to wash your face?'

'That bad?'

She shrugged. 'It could be worse.'

I slipped off my jacket and winced. 'Tomorrow. I'll take a hot bath in the morning. Or afternoon. Whenever I wake up.' If I had anything to do with it, it would be at least afternoon. I remember the first time I got shot. It burned. The working over I received from these heavies, however, brought out a new orchestra of pain. Professionals, I guess. They knew how to give a lot of lasting suffering without leaving any permanent markers. Forget pointing them out in a line-up.

Black clothes, black Docs, grim faces and heavy hands. Yeah, it was a lot to go on.

I wriggled out of my trousers with Jinx's help. 'Just leave me. Tomorrow. I'll feel better tomorrow.' I pulled open the drawer to paw through the contents.

'You might want to be careful what you take,' Saunders cautioned, hovering near the door.

'I know my limits. And in case you haven't noticed, I'm in a good bit of pain here. I deserve a little vacation from my senses.' I did a good pick-n-mix of oxy and sleepers. A little whisky to wash it down sounded tempting, but I figured it was better to stick with water. 'I'll be better tomorrow.'

'You want me to call… someone?' Saunders frowned.

I considered this as I lay back on my pillow. 'You might put a word in Coburn's ear. Just to let him know it's not all in my head.' Said head screamed for a 'shut up now' order. I closed my eyes. 'What's left of it anyway.'

'All right. I'll check on you later.'

'Yeah, okay,' I muttered, the beating itself already the best sleep inducer. I wanted to hurry that fuzzy feeling along and fade to black. Before I did, I heard Saunders say to Jinx,

'Keep an eye on him.'

What was I going to do? Sneak out and join the circus when she wasn't looking? Sleep sidled into my bed like Virginia Grahame in a slinky negligee and wrapped itself around my aching form until at last the blissful abyss opened before me.

I awoke with a groan. And Peaches, who sat on the edge of my bed as if she had taken up residence there. 'You don't half sleep,' she said with a yawn.

I snorted, feeling anew the stiffness and pain that wracked my frame just from that tiny movement. I drew in a slow deep breath then reached out my arm to paw at the drawer in the nightstand to rescue a little more respite from the mosaic of agony that filled my muscles and limbs. 'You couldn't give us a hand here,' I rasped at Peaches, feeling my meagre strength escape me.

'Sorry, mate,' she said shrugging. 'Incorporeal. I learned that word here. I am 'incorporeal' and thus I cannot have a presence in the material world.'

'Some do,' I argued as I lay panting from the exertion.

'Oh yeah, like that one Patrick Swayze movie where he

saves his wife, what's-er-name from that other bloke. The old one married to Ashton Kutcher. You know!'

'I don't even know that name,' I said steeling myself for a second assault. I got the drawer open and grabbed the right bottle. Olly olly oxy free. 'You mean *Ghost*, ' I said after I'd dry-swallowed my salvation.

Peaches winced. Actually winced. 'We don't use that word. It's considered rude.'

I closed my eyes. 'What's the right term then? Spook? Spectre? No one's mentioned it to me before.'

'You don't much listen though, do you, I expect.' Peaches huffed, looking irritable and bored. The afterlife did not suit her.

'I listen, but I'm a busy man.'

'You don't look very busy.'

'Peaches, I got beat to a bloody pulp last night. I think I deserve a little break.'

She turned and peered at me. 'Huh, I guess you did. Wow, your face looks like mince! Maybe you should do something about that.'

'I am,' I muttered as I slipped back into the depths of my duvet.

When I surfaced once more I blinked a few times and then groaned. I groped in the drawer for some helpers. As I choked them down I realised it was quiet. No Peaches, no Saunders, no Jinx. The silence seemed eerie. My hand patted around on the nightstand until I found my granddad's pocket watch. The only timepiece I know that would work reliably in this house.

Three o'clock. I squinted at the shaded window: was that ante or post? I couldn't be sure. Either it was the middle of the night or the middle of a very grey afternoon I really wasn't certain. But I definitely felt the call of the wild—or at least the commode.

Bracing myself, I rolled to the edge of the bed and gingerly dropped my feet to the floor. The pain made me gasp so I waited a little while to try to lift my torso upright. Babyface's lads had earned their pay. There was probably some NHS-recommended technique for getting out of bed when badly injured, perhaps with a broken rib, that my local health practitioner could have offered me had I gone to see her.

In the end I used my arms to try to lift me instead of the usual back muscles. You never know just how complicated the structure of the human body is until it suffers severe pain. Then you know every little bone and muscle and how they're connected.

At least my bladder stopped hurting once I emptied it. I thought of returning to bed but the lure of a nice hot bath seduced me. I flipped on the boiler then rummaged around under the sink, sucking in a little at the unexpected pain when I first bent over, but I found the gigantic ancient box of Epsom salts that Auntie Vera swore by for her various aches and pains. It was nearly empty but that was just as well as I doubtless couldn't have lifted it were it still full.

I stood woozily swaying while the bath filled, wondering if I would ever be able to get back out of the tub once I was in. *I'll think about that when I get there.* Stripped of my remaining clothes, I sidled into the tub and at once groaned with a weird combination of pain and pleasure. It was very nearly sexual.

'Hot bath, will you marry me?'

It's entirely possible that the drugs had kicked in.

I lolled in the water until it became tepid, my fingers had pruned and the pain had subsided to a dull roar. It took a bit of ingenuity to hoist myself back out of the porcelain womb, but I managed it at last, did a poor job of towelling the worst of me and slipped on my old dressing gown. I could hear a kettle calling my name.

As I limped down the corridor, I could also hear other voices. When I stepped through the kitchen door I found they belonged to Saunders and Coburn.

'You look much better,' Saunders said, the wrinkle on her brow making me think she was surprised to find it so.

'You look like shit,' my former partner said, pushing his chair back and looking me up and down and shaking his head at the same time. Didn't half make me dizzy, all that movement. 'No, you look like the shit that's left over when all the real shit has been shovelled up.'

'Is the kettle on?' I said, groaning as I eased into chair, making an even bigger show of my pain in the vain attempt to elicit some sympathy. Saunders didn't answer but flipped it on and got me a big mug from the cupboard, its design a testimony to Auntie Vera's addiction to a certain hazelnut spread.

'So tell me about it,' Coburn said with an air of indulgence once he'd run out of insults for my kisser. 'You know what guys did this to you?'

'Raphaelita set me up, so I guess they were Babyface's heavies. I don't know. Maybe he figured I was getting something for free but I was just asking her some questions. Ta.' Saunders set the Nutella mug down and I inhaled the comforting aroma of the tea.

'You should see a doctor now,' she tutted.

I shrugged and then winced. 'Jinx can tape me up. He's had plenty of practice. Where is he?'

'You needed bread.'

'Bread?'

She nodded. 'And something to put on it. And tea. And sugar. Do you always eat takeaway?'

'What's wrong with a good curry?'

She shrugged and busied herself pouring another cup for Coburn. He pressed me for details of my attackers and I did my best to reconstruct the evening.

'Black clothes and Docs,' Saunders interrupted.

'Yeah, far as I could tell.'

'Don't you think they might be Dockmuir's men instead?'

'Wha?' My brain seemed a tad bit sluggish, but a light had begun to glimmer. 'Dockmuir's men? You think?'

'Well, they do rather sound like the same guys who loaded us into the van.'

'Loaded you—what?' Coburn suddenly looked a lot more interested. 'Dockmuir? What have you been doing that you didn't tell me about?'

'I didn't do anything,' I muttered.

'Dockmuir had us over for a little chat,' Saunders offered.

'You didn't mention that,' Coburn said, looking a bit miffed.

'We aren't partners anymore in case you didn't notice that empty desk next to yours all this time,' I said, feeling a little smug and superior.

'It's not empty,' Coburn said evenly. 'Riley moved into it. Doing grand work.'

I snorted, which I immediately regretted because my ribs reminded me of their delicate state. 'Grand work.'

'Well, as you say, we aren't partners anymore.' Coburn sniffed and sipped his tea.

'If you boys are done waving those things at each other,' Saunders said to finally break the silence, 'Can we get back to this problem?'

'What problem?' I did the tea sipping thing, too. It was a good ploy to stall for time.

'If Dockmuir is roughing you up, don't you think that's a problem?'

I had to admit she was probably right. Of course I didn't have to admit it right away. Damn her anyway. 'Well, let's not immediately jump to conclusions. Maybe they just *looked* like Dockmuir's men.'

'So maybe Babyface is working with Dockmuir—or he's got a hold over him somehow,' Saunders suggested without paying attention to my weak attempt at back-pedalling.

'I don't know of any link between them before,' Coburn mused, rubbing his chin. He hadn't shaved that day it appeared. Not like my partner to get sloppy unless he had been working long hours. 'Babyface was always his own man, steered clear of the bigger bosses by sticking to his own turf.'

'Maybe Dockmuir's just using him to get to us. Or at least him.' She looked at me with a curiously objective view, which made her seem suddenly unfriendly.

'I don't suppose we could go back to the view that Babyface just wanted payback for me taking up some of Raphaelita's time?'

'Don't think so,' Coburn said and then sighed.

'I take it there's a reason.' And it didn't sound good.

'We fished Babyface out of the Thames near the Tilbury Docks earlier today.'

'By his socks?' I suggested, but neither of them laughed. 'Drowned?'

'Shot. But then he got hung up on the lines from a fishing boat and then run up into a propeller, which sliced him up a fair bit. We were lucky his face remained recognisable.'

'That would have made him happy.'

Saunders gave me such a look. Oxford should poach her to teach meaningful looks and glances. It would improve the lives of the undergraduates.

'It's true. He was the most vain man I ever met.'

'More so than the goat boy?' Coburn said, obviously doubting me.

'Way more than the goat boy! C'mon!'

'I don't think I even want to know who you're talking about,' Saunders said, edging away from us just a little.

'You *really* don't want to know why he got his name, either.' Coburn shook his head.

'Well, what about Dockmuir? You think he whacked Babyface?'

'Whacked? What are you? A gangster now?' My former partner had an unpleasant sneer.

'Hey, do you think Raphaelita is all right?' The thought gave me an unpleasant turn. The odds were that she had been offed too, or else slated to be. 'You think some of the lads could go check on her?'

Coburn's face became serious at once. He fished in his pocket for his phone and called the station. 'They'll check but I'd be real surprised if she isn't gone, either permanent or because she got wind of Babyface's early demise.' He spoke a few curt orders down the line, put the phone back in his coat pocket and stood up. 'I've got a few things to look into.' He nodded at Saunders who nodded back. 'Don't get yourself entangled with this fool.'

'Who you calling fool?' I said with a superior laugh and immediately wished I hadn't, as it made my ribs ache.

'And you, try not to get killed. I don't know why it should matter anyway, but I ask you nonetheless.'

I smothered several wisecracks and stuck to saying, 'Stay safe, partner.'

'I'm not your partner,' Coburn said, then slapped his hat on his head and headed out. But he didn't say it with the usual exasperation so I thought maybe he had mellowed a bit toward me.

'Am I going to find out what happened between you two?' Saunders asked as she flipped on the kettle again.

'I hope not.' I groaned again as I tried to rise out of the chair.

'What do you want? I can get it.'

'He don't want nothing, he's just whinging.' Peaches sat on the edge of the table, one sandaled foot dangling as she snapped her gum.

'Why are you here to plague me again, Peaches?' Saunders shot me a look, then went back to pouring two fresh cups.

'I was waiting for him to leave, we all were.'

'Why? You crowd in the rest of the time and yammer on.' I wasn't feeling up to a round robin Rosabel just then.

Peaches got a funny look then. If I had to find a word for it, I would have said spooked, which seemed more than a tad ironic. 'He's got some strong mojo around him. None of us like to get too near.'

'Coburn does?' News to me.

'Does what?'

I forgot that Saunders wasn't always hearing what I was hearing. 'Peaches says he's got some powerful protection around him, keeps her lot away. Now that I think about it, that would explain a few things.' And why I could never get him to acknowledge even a hint of what I had to put up with from the ineffable realms. Hmmm, who'd be putting the mojo around him? It couldn't be Sylvia, whom all the swains adored. His impossibly lovely wife that made everyone wonder what she saw in him that we missed?—she didn't seem the type at all. Too busy running the world.

Then again, you never knew what talents people had that they kept well hid. 'Say, Peaches, you didn't see Babyface hanging around out there?'

'The singer?' She looked genuinely surprised.

'Singer? There's a singer with that stupid name? No, the pimp. Got knocked off his socks at the Tilbury Docks.'

'I'm unfamiliar with the gentleman,' she said with admirable disdain. 'You going to do your job now?'

'My job?' I took the mug gratefully from the nonplussed Saunders who sat opposite me, waiting I suppose for some translation of the conversation. 'My job is figuring out who's trying to make my life miserable.'

'And me dead,' Peaches said, 'which I think might be a little more of a pressing issue here. But I meant all the folk what want to speak with you. You got something of a line up waiting in the other room.' She jerked her thumb over her shoulder.

'I'm not sure I'm up to it,' I grumbled.

'Yeah, well, maybe that Babyface is there,' Peaches said. Oooh, such a practiced temptress—she knew the way to a man's weak spot. She had a point, however. One I couldn't afford to overlook.

'What?' Saunders asked at last as I gave a huge sigh of acquiescence. I knew it really got up her nose when I spoke to people who weren't there and she hated to admit just how much, so she had to be really exasperated to ask.

I really ought to be nicer to her.

'Peaches has pointed out that among the dead currently thronging for my attention in the other room, we *might* just find Babyface who *might* be able to turn into black and white the situation somewhat.'

'The other room,' Saunders said, 'The megaphone room. The dead.'

'They don't get any deader,' I agreed.

'You feel up to something like that?' The dismay on her face spoke volumes. I had carefully avoided looking at my reflection in the bathroom mirror. I knew how bad I felt, but it finally struck me to wonder how bad I looked. I certainly felt as if I ought to be lying in a bank of pillows stacked upon a raft of soft duvets with a few fluffy bunnies on the top of it, tucked round by some cherubs' diaphanous drapery.

Lacking same I might as well log a little time in the luminiferous ether to keep my mind off the pain, which the chemicals kept at arm's length but did not dispel. It's not as if I had to do any heavy lifting, except of myself as I discovered when I tried to rise from my seat. 'Give us a hand, will ye?'

Saunders moved forward to yank on my arm. 'No, the other one, it hurts less. I think.' Switching her target, Saunders helped me stagger out of the chair and crush her a little too precipitously. I winced from the pain, she from my sudden proximity, I suspect. I had time to notice she smelled of spice and flowers before she righted me a little too enthusiastically and stepped away.

'Do you want me… to help?'

'Help how?' I asked and then felt at once like kicking myself, which would prove a challenge even if I weren't wracked with pain. 'I mean, you can watch.'

'Watch?'

I grimaced. Let her think it was the pain. 'I meant you can help me keep up with all the comments and requests and things and you know.'

Saunders regarded me with those too serious eyes and that judging brow. She didn't say anything, but when I staggered along the corridor to the parlour her light footsteps trailed mine.

Peaches waited inside, perched on the edge of the table, her sandaled toes swinging again. 'You got quite the queue here. I been calling for this Babyface geezer, but he don't seem to be about. Others are champin' at the proverbial bit.'

I eased myself down into the captain's chair with a little groan that was not at all put up for Saunders' benefit. 'Could you grab that notepad?'

Saunders slid the pad across to me and took a seat at the table. I could feel her nervous awareness rise. She couldn't see anything in the room, but she certainly seemed to sense it. Must be all the hair.

If I squinted I could see their shapes. They hovered restless and eager. I figured I should give it a go and see if Babyface were around. 'I am seeking Babyface who I understand has recently joined the realms of the veil.' I paused to ascertain whether there was any answer. 'Babyface, I know you tried to have me beat to a pulp, but all things considered you had it worse, so no grudge, eh?'

'Anything?' Saunders asked after another pause.

'Not a sausage. Peaches, you don't see anything, er, anyone answering?'

'Not a peep.'

I sighed. 'Damn.'

'Maybe,' Saunders said hesitatingly, as if reluctant to suggest that she had even the remotest particle of faith in any of this, 'you need something of his to call him.'

'Yeah, like when you tried to call the previous missus for me,' Peaches agreed. 'Makes sense. A connection.'

'What about this lot then?' I asked crossly. I had to admit that I thought the personal item thing a bit of a razzle dazzle for the punters not a real thing after all. A bit rum to be caught not knowing my own game. 'They don't even seem to need an invitation, let alone a personal item.'

'I thought you did this for a living, don't you know all about it now?' Saunders asked nonplussed.

'He's been faking it so long he don't know what's real,' Peaches laughed.

'Stow it, Peaches.'

'Ms. Weiner to you, 'cause you're nasty,' Peaches sang.

'What?' Saunders asked, probably wondering what she was missing.

'I have often mistaken the tools for the truths and vice versa,' I admitted. 'But maybe there's something to the idea of getting a personal belonging.'

'Do you think you can?'

I shrugged and recalled at once how even that reminded me of my injuries. 'We can start with Raphaelita's place, make sure she's okay and maybe mooch around and find something else, maybe something that belonged to him.'

'And in the meantime?'

I shoved the pad of A4 toward her, leaned forward and accepted the inevitable. 'You take notes, I'll translate.' Then I opened my mind up to the mystical realms and got ready for a good old natter. Inevitably, the hubbub overwhelmed at first and I had to get a little shirty or I would have been babbling myself in no time.

The dead: they lose all sense of time.

The upshot of course was that I was even more knackered by the end of an hour and instead of heading off to find Raphaelita I only wanted to find the sandman. 'Just a nap,' I yawned to Saunders as Jinx taped up my ribs as gently as he could manage.

'We can go without you,' Saunders suggested.

I looked at her earnest face. Why did it have to be such a nice earnest face? 'I don't think that's too wise. She doesn't know you. She'll be cagey even if she is there, which she might not be.'

'I could take Jinx along.'

'He's busy,' I said crossly even though he was already nodding. 'Just leave it. We've waited this long, we can wait a bit longer.' My eyelids were screaming for release and my body sang the same song, harmonising on the pain side of things. Time to sprinkle a little more fairy dust on my poor bones.

'What do I do with all this?' Saunders held up the pad of A4 covered in her scratchings.

'Your handwriting's worse than mine.'

'And?'

'Just leave them here. We'll do... something with them later.' Saunders gave me her patented raised eyebrow but I didn't allow it to intimidate me. 'If you want to do any investigating into those stories, be my guest, but you'll probably find more questions than answers, I suspect.'

'Like who they are.'

'A big one that, eh?' I turned to limp off to my room, wondering if it would look bad to let Jinxy assist me. 'If you want to dig though, there's your garden, Peter Rabbit.'

'How do you know I'm not Jemima Puddle-Duck?'

I barked with laughter, which made me nearly collapse, but I rasped out, 'No hat.' I was rewarded with an amused look from Saunders that somehow seemed worthwhile as Jinx manoeuvered me along the corridor to my stately abode. I'd like to say sleep did not require chemical enhancements but I wasn't about to take chances there.

A fitful hour or two later, I struggled back up to consciousness. Some demented sort of evil, sentient toadstools haunted my dream like a Disney film gone horribly awry or maybe they just are that awful. I hadn't seen one since I was a wee tot and had to be removed screaming from the theatre. Not sure what it was that had frightened me. I think it was Snow White's piercing voice. The toadstools in my dreams were soft and suffocating, like floating pillows. They left me with a vague sense of unease.

I rambled down to the kitchen and found Saunders and Jinx in a deep conference in the kitchen, which is to say she was jabbering and he was listening with something more than his usual mild regard. 'What's the rumpus?' I said grandly as I groaned into a chair.

'We're working,' Saunders said a little shortly. Clearly I had worn out the sympathy card. 'There are some weird things among all this gibberish.'

'What gibberish?'

She thrust the pad at me, several circles now drawn upon it and heavy lines connecting them. 'This.'

I stared at his scratching and the circles and the lines and wondered if I had overdone the self-medicating again. No, it was definitely gibberish. 'I don't see what you're trying to show me. I know you made circles and lines but it looks even more rubbishy than it did before.'

Saunders snatched back the pad with noise of irritation. 'You're blind as well as dumb.'

'I'm not the dumb one and ow,' I said before sticking my finger in my mouth. 'Paper cut!'

'Didn't you wonder why there were even more people hanging around in the dead room than before?'

I winced, still sucking at the finger. 'Don't call it the dead room.'

'What do you call it?'

'The parlour. You know, paper cuts really hurt.'

She ignored my whimpering. 'Whatever you call it, it's getting a lot of people who are not from around here.'

'South London is a melting pot at the crossroads of the world,' I said with a certain amount of civic pride.

'I don't mean that. A lot of them don't seem to have any connection with London at all. But a lot of them use the same words over and over.' She tapped at the pad with her finger.

'Words like what?'

'Trapped is one.' She pointed to the word in several places, flipping the page over to the next one, too.

'Well,' I said trying to harrumph with authority, 'When souls get trapped between existences—'

'Not that kind of trapped.' Saunders pointed back at the pad. 'They say someone's put them here.'

'Paranoia,' I said, though I was beginning to get the prickly feeling on the back of my neck that I hated so much.

'Maybe, but there's this, too.' Saunders held the pad up so there was no mistaking it. 'White rabbit. A few different times, different people it seemed. I was writing so fast while you were rambling on, but even so I noticed the repetition. Didn't you?'

'Say Jinxy, I could murder a cuppa.' I hoped my voice didn't waver. He nodded and got up, though I could tell he'd rather have stuck in the middle of the conversation.

'Didn't you though?' Saunders insisted.

'I don't notice anything when I'm communing with the dead,' I said without any attempt to bury the irritation I felt. 'I'm in the zone like the players say. I don't know what's passing through my mouth. I'm just channelling what's there.'

'Sounds creepy. Kind of horrifying.'

I shifted and groaned a little more. 'No more than watching a movie or a play. You step aside and let the story be told, get caught up in things. It can be entertaining.'

'I don't think I'd like it,' Saunders said, shaking her head slowly.

'Well, nobody's asking you to.'

'What's got up your nose?'

I snorted. 'You have.'

'I thought you wanted to sort this mystery.'

'Thank you, Miss Marple. Or would that be Jane Tennison?' She did favour the fabulous Dame now that I thought about it and was long sprints away from any genteel old biddyhood. I noticed Jinxy was watching the back and forth as if he were at Wimbledon. 'How's that cuppa coming along?'

'Aren't we going to Raphaelita's now?' Saunders champed at the bit when she wanted something. I found it inconvenient. I was accustomed to more latitude in my day.

'You wouldn't make a man rush off without a little boost?'

'I assumed you took care of that already.'

I could feel the ice in her voice freeze my skin. 'I was badly beaten just recently if I'm not terribly mistaken.' I held out the arm with the purple welts on it for good measure, which made it her turn to wince. I wanted to nip in the bud her lazy assumption that I was always on the dust. It wasn't fair! 'I think a little something to ease the pain might be called for.'

'That sounds suspiciously like 'or any other reason why',' Saunders retorted, but sat down again nonetheless. Jinx set a steaming cup in front of her first, then me and then poured one for himself.

Homey.

Later, as if joined at the hip, the three of us wandered off to see if we could scare up Raphaelita—or rather, *not* scare her. A gentle knock on her door revealed it to have been left open. After a moment's blinking conferral with my colleagues, I cautiously pushed it open with a couple of fingers.

We released a collective sigh of relief upon seeing no corpse sprawled inside. A quick reconnoitre of the tiny toilet also stamped it body-free. Of course that didn't mean she wasn't dead.

'Do you think—?'

I shook my head, at first just because I didn't want to think it. Sure, Raphaelita had set me up for the beating, but I couldn't really bear a grudge. I always liked her. She was just doing her job. However, as I looked around the flat—it really wasn't much more than a bedsit—I became more certain that she had got away. Things were messy, which wasn't like her at all. All her clothes were gone; they were the tools of her trade but to roughnecks, they'd just be so many dresses and stockings. 'Her clothes are gone. She must have packed them up and high-tailed it out of here.'

'Unless she was kidnapped,' Saunders said, examining a set of souvenir spoons from Scotland as if they might hold some vital clue beyond jam, jute and journalism.

I smothered an annoyed sound. '*All* her clothes are gone. All. Kidnappers might grab some of her clothes, but they're *all* gone.' I tried not to sound smug. It wasn't easy.

'You seem to know a lot about it,' a flat voice opined from the doorway.

I groaned. I couldn't help it. Saunders got that hunted look that I used to know so well. 'What are you doing here, Burnsie?'

'I might ask you the same,' Burns sneered back. 'Fabulous to see you here as it might be.'

'Righteo.' I was stalling and avoiding Saunders' eye, because my heart sank into my boots as soon as I saw Burns. It wasn't just that he was widely suspected to be a very dirty boy indeed. That would explain his being added to the case when my ex-partner had been taken off it. Burns was even dodgier than that. He was known for his cruelty on any pretext but more than that he was unsettling. It was said round the shop that he managed to be so slippery that even his guvnor didn't even know where he really lived. The tabs had floated his name for a few shady disappearances but even the newshound boyos didn't have a clue to just how much went awry with his unseen help—or so my old sergeant had whispered to me. None of my colleagues liked to find him in the same room, but just as soon as you spotted him, he was likely to be gone.

Slippery as an eel.

'You do know you're interfering with a crime scene,' he said with an expression so smug he might have nicked it off the Cheshire Cat.

'Crime?' I said, modulating my dulcet tones to express surprise. 'Has something happened to Raphaelita? We were hoping to get her to come along to the pictures tonight, weren't we, gang?'

Jinx and Saunders nodded, looking warily at Burns. Himself laughed, but also seemed to find that a bit of a quandary. He couldn't give away the game unless he knew how much we knew. 'Pull the other one.'

'I assume it's got bells. And I thought that jingle in your pocket just meant you were glad to see me.'

'Fuck off, Jawbone.' Said without rancour. Said also without any friendliness.

'So what's the crime in this scene?' I asked, genuinely curious what he might say.

Burns stared at me for a long moment, then smiled that reptilian smile. 'You're interfering with an officer in the conduct of his duty. That's all you need know. Maybe I need to take you in.'

'Are you getting this all down?' I said, turning to Saunders on inspiration. She stared at me, flummoxed. 'Or is your digital recorder on?' I stole a glance at Burns. He had no smile now. 'We don't want to get the details wrong. So much depends on a red wheel barrow.'

'Fuck you, Jawbone,' Burns said, the rancour very much included in the price of the meal. But I saw doubt in his face, too. The last thing he ever needed was press. Against his whole raison d'être that.

'We were just going anyway. Gotta catch that curtain.' I nodded toward the exit and Jinx escorted Saunders toward the door. 'You take care now, Burnsie. Don't be working those long hours. It'll give you eye strain.'

'Keep yappin' and you'll get another working over, Jawbone.' He just couldn't resist. I tipped an imaginary stove-pipe to him as I sashayed out the door. But I was genuinely grateful to the mug. He had given me a little information. If he knew about me getting roughed up, this business came from inside.

And I was in a lot deeper than I had guessed. Dirty cops plus an immoral mogul spelt trouble.

'So, where to?' Saunders broke into my reverie, leaving me vaguely discombobulated. Or maybe it was the effects of the beating. Or the dust. Who could say?

'I really don't know.' Sometimes the truth was not only simplest, it was also the easiest to remember. 'The trail's gone a bit cold, eh?'

Jinx harrumphed.

I flushed. 'No, we're not going to the pictures, Jinx. That was just a ruse. Although—' Wondered what was playing at Waterloo. I liked to go to the big 3D spectacles and just groove to the shiny lights and colours. Insufficient supplies for everyone, however.

'We really need to work on this,' Saunders urged. 'It's getting more and more dangerous.'

'You got an idea how to do that? Because I'm kind of stuck for an angle at present.' I walked along as fast as I could, which I realised wasn't all that fast being as I still hurt like hell all over. I patted my pocket and found myself reassured by its contents.

'What about all the dead folks and the connections they made?' She was like a dog with a bone on this.

'Connections?' I did my best to sound as dismissive as possible. Not sure why. It could be entirely possible that I was just being a berk about it. 'We have a few words in little circles. Trapped? Who wouldn't feel trapped if they got caught in a loop in the ether? They just need to pass on to the next plane.'

Even Jinxy grunted at that, as if to suggest I used to be a better liar. Or maybe I was extrapolating a little too much from the noise he had made.

91

'What about all the mentions of 'white rabbit'? You can't brush that off so easily.' Saunders got top marks in persistence. 'There's something weird going on here.'

'Maybe we should talk it over in the pub.' A fine specimen of the type appeared before us as if by magic. I had just about stepped over the threshold when she pulled me up short.

'I found some potentially interesting things in my research at the BL,' Saunders said, her voice flat, as if it went against the grain to give up the ace in the hole she had up her sleeve.

'Good,' I said, 'We can take a look at it while we sip a few thirst slayers.'

'I left the folder at the house.'

Heaven preserve those who stand in the way of a pub outing. But I was enough of a gentleman not to hit a girl. Or woman. I did want to hit someone. However, I was in too much pain to hit anyone with anything resembling effectiveness.

Homeward we sped—well, when I say sped, we jumped on the 59 and took our sweet time getting there. And I was walking even slower by the time we got off the bus as my limbs had stiffened as we sat there reading discarded tabs. I didn't mind the retrograde politics so much—after all, I hadn't paid for the rags—but the fall in quality of page three lovelies, or at least my noticing of it, suggested I was getting old.

That was depressing.

Back at the house we parked ourselves around the kitchen table as Jinxy made tea and Saunders gathered up her research. 'Criminy, you've got manila folders?'

She gave me the stink eye. 'Some of us like to keep things organised.'

I stared balefully at the pile of folders. At least I think it was balefully. I'm not even sure what 'baleful' means, but it seemed to fit the context. Maybe I should look it up. 'How much of this is actually useful?'

Saunders ignored me and opened one of the folders. 'There are people disappearing—'

'There are always people disappearing. Trust me, I used to work on their cases. Endless cases of dead faces.'

Saunders threw a few photocopied pictures at me. 'These aren't your usual missing persons. We're not talking vulnerable people on the edge or rich teens or junkies. Professionals, seemingly well-adjusted members of society, even a couple of your mates, police officers. Gone—not dead, not found.'

I looked at the pictures and one young woman with a business suit seemed particularly accusatory. Or was it familiar? 'Look, I know these kinds of stories. People who seem your regular neighbour next door, boring as day old bread, no surprises, but then something happens. You never know what. They step out in front of a car and see their lives flash before them. Or they meet the person they think should have been with all along, but they're fifteen years into a dead marriage.

'And then they decide that maybe they took a wrong turn or stepped through the wrong door, and they think to themselves that maybe it's not too late. Maybe they can start again, only it's a little tricky with the kids and the mortgage and the job, so they scarper off. If they're smart, they try to clear the way with a fake death or suicide situation, but most of them just fade into Nowheresville and leave a lot of questions and friends and family wondering what they really ever knew about this person.

'And you know the worst thing?' I waved down Saunders' attempt to interrupt. 'The thing is when you catch up to them, they're living the same old boring life with the same sort of family or situation and convincing themselves it was all worthwhile and they don't miss a thing. But they do, they do.'

'You're a cynical bastard,' Saunders said with what I hoped might be admiration.

'Oh fuck me,' I said. 'I know where that woman's from.' I peered at the young woman in the business suit again.

'You do?'

I nodded slowly. The image swam back to me slowly through memory, vision, whatever it was that filled my head. One of the throng, she was, gathering around the room, murmuring into the megaphone of my ears. 'Trapped'—yes, surely, and 'white rabbit'? Was that there, too?

As if bidden by my thoughts I felt the unpleasant and slightly tickling sensation prickling at the back of my skull. Things would go easier if I moved to the other room, but I felt an irrational wave of annoyance wash over me.

'Well?' Saunders stared at me. I'm sure she saw something happening on my face. I took a moment to consider what she thought it might be and whether she had any estimation of me whatsoever. Not that it should matter, but somehow it did. Damn her anyway. I was doing fine before she came along to mess up my life.

'I think I'm going to go to the parlour.' I got up, gritting my teeth because every time I sat for a while my whole body stiffened up. Have you ever been punched in the kidney? It's an effective blow. Hurts like hell for days but doesn't leave a mark. A favourite of police forces and fascist armies the world over. My attackers had made good use of the technique. Between the rib and the kidney there was maybe an inch of space, but it held a world of hurt.

'Do you, er, want help?'

'Yeah,' I said, taking in the genuine look of concern she had in those soft brown eyes. I had thought they were green before. Maybe they changed colours or maybe she had contacts. 'But we've already established you can't lift me.' Jinxy moved over but I waved him away. 'Joking, mate. I'll hobble.'

'How about taking notes?'

I sucked in some air at a surprise hurt as turned. 'I'm guessing you wouldn't want to help me undress?'

Saunders raised one firm eyebrow looking very Bacall. 'That help your contact with the other realms?'

'No, not really. Just a pathetic excuse to get naked.'

She laughed which I hadn't heard often enough these days. But she didn't immediately say no, either.

'Not going for it?'

'I've seen you naked.'

I choked. 'When?!'

'When we first met. Don't you remember?' Saunders grinned. '*I* remember.'

'You do?' I could feel bits of me wilting considerably. It wasn't a good feeling. 'Ah, impressive eh?'

She lifted the other eyebrow. Saunders could lift eyebrows for England. 'What do you think?'

'Can I defer comment until I confer with counsel?'

'Let's just get things rolling in the de—parlour, all right?'

'Right.' She got her pad and I brought my mug and we sat ourselves down at the table. And *she* was there. In her business suit and all. 'Hello.'

'I see you. You see me?' Her words came unevenly but I could see her outline gradually taking shape.

'I see you. What do you want to tell us?'

'Did you find them?'

'Find who?'

'I left word... wasn't it you? I know I spoke with someone here... recently... Is it Thursday?' Her voice wavered.

'I couldn't tell you what day it is,' I said truthfully but as gently as possible. 'But we did indeed speak.' I glanced over at Saunders, who flipped pages of the yellow A4 pad hastily, then folded the loose ones back and thrust the appropriate page before me. She had underlined 'young woman in sharp suit' and had circled 'white rabbit' and 'trapped' but saw there was more scribbled down in Saunders' scratchy hand.

'I don't know where I am,' the young woman said, her voice faltering with confusion.

'You're safe here with us,' I said, not sure I was being entirely truthful, but somehow compelled to be reassuring if I could manage it. The curse of our land, I suppose. 'What can you tell us about the white rabbit?'

'The rabbit runs,' she said vaguely, wading into the middle of the big oak table as if it were water. 'It ran over me.'

'Ran over you?' This was a common problem with the deceased. They spoke gibberish, forgot what they were on about, forgot their native tongue, forgot what it meant to be human and all. 'The rabbit ran over you?'

'Yes, the rabbit ran over me.'

This was getting us nowhere. I looked over at Saunders. I tried the eyebrow thing at her. Should have known better.

'Try another tack,' she whispered.

I shrugged and sighed. 'Where were you when this happened?'

'Headquarters,' she replied, willowy and more insubstantial. Not a good sign.

'Work headquarters?'

'No, the warren.'

Now we were getting somewhere. 'The rabbit warren?'

'Yes, the others—what happened to them? Are they all right?'

I didn't know how to answer so I just said, 'I think so. I haven't seen any of them around here anyway.'

'Where's here?' The look on her face—it wasn't quite suspicion, more worry—and a good bit of fear. She looked around her as if she could see the room. I was never sure what they saw when they were hereabouts. I always fancied I was a shimmering light in the darkness but maybe that was Auntie Vera's teaching again.

'You're visiting my house,' I said, trying to lead her away from that line of questioning. 'Where is the warren? Have I been there?'

She looked around some more and I was beginning to think she wouldn't answer me at all, but at last she said, 'By the river.'

'Which river?'

'There's only one river, isn't there?'

'Some would doubtless agree,' I said. 'Where by the river? Inland or nearer the coast, or somewhere in between?'

'Down toward the towers, the docks.' She grew even more insubstantial. I'd better pick up the pace.

'Tower Bridge?' I tried. 'Or Tilbury Docks?'

'Canaries,' she said becoming more and more inaudible. 'I remember canaries, or some birds...'

'Canary Wharf?' I hoped that was right and not just a guess. I didn't hear an answer though for she had faded away.

I shuddered involuntarily at an imagined chill. 'Well, that was a bust.'

'Not entirely.' Saunders shook her head. 'We learned there's a warren. The rabbit has a home.'

I considered this. 'By the river, maybe Canary Wharf? I suppose it's something. Mighty thin however.'

'Thin is better than none which is what we had before.' She flipped through the pages of the pad, staring at the words with her laser vision. I wondered if she could see through the pages. I wondered if that's how she saw through me. 'If we reconsider the others' comments in that light, maybe we can put together more of a picture of things, find this warren.'

'Look we don't even know if this 'warren' is a real place. You don't want to go putting too much stock in what dead folks say. Sometimes they're confused. Or confusing. They don't see the world the way we do anymore. What is it, Jinx?'

Jinx cocked his head toward the kitchen, signalling tea was ready. We picked up and moved back to the next room. Just as well: the pricklings along the back of my skull were beginning again and I didn't really want to deal with them just now.

Had to admit, I missed Peaches a bit, but all things considered it might be best not to see too much of her. 'What's that?'

'Lentil and bacon soup,' Saunders said with something like satisfaction in her voice. I knew it must be her doing. I looked at Jinxy. He shrugged. Saunders looked at the two of us with amusement. 'It's got bacon.'

I sighed and sat down. 'Nutritious food will just be a shock to my system. You don't know what you have wrought.' Nonetheless I started to eat, sopping up the soup with some good grainy bread that smelled like a bakery in the morning. There just might be something to this healthy eating business. Nonetheless my innards were making gurgling sounds that suggested the change might be too violent.

Saunders busied herself with the manila folders between sips of soup. She was about the neatest eater I ever saw. Some lines from Chaucer tried to creep back into memory but they remained elusive. So much for Sister Honoria's ruler. Its blows remained vivid. I wondered if I counted up the blows I had received in this life just how much they would total, like guessing the number of pickled eggs in a jar. But without a prize for it in the end.

'Here's another mention of the towers and the docks,' Saunders said breaking into my idle thoughts. 'And here, the warren. And here, too.'

'Okay, so maybe it could be a real place.' I could admit when I was wrong. Sometimes. 'But where is it? I guessed Canary Wharf but that's a shot in the dark. Get a map of the Thames—it could be anywhere along there. Towers and wharves?'

'Towers and docks,' Saunders corrected.

'Hickory dickory docks, Tilbury socks—it could be anywhere.'

'You don't seem too interested all of the sudden.' Saunders gave me an uncomfortable searching look.

'Not all of the sudden. I've not been too interested at all. I just want to go back to my quiet life and forget all this.' I was much more sanguine with a full belly, healthy food or not. 'I don't know why I should keep poking my nose into this business when a wide variety of people have made it clear that my nose and the rest of me is not welcome in this business.'

'No desire to see Dockmuir brought down now?'

I waved a careless hand. 'Live and let live, eh?'

Saunders snorted. 'You are still under investigation for murder, or did you forget that, too?'

That was a low blow. I had conveniently forgotten that particular fact. Consequently I sulked and refused to speak any further while I examined my miserable situation. Silence reigned for a time while I scowled and Saunders shuffled through the papers while Jinx helped himself to the last of the soup, scraping the bottom of the pot with his enthusiasm.

I heard the phone begin to ring. The summons from the foyer could easily be ignored on the best of days. This was not the best of days.

'Aren't you going to get that?' Saunders said at last.

'Nope.'

'Why not?'

'Last time I took a phone call it led to my being badly beaten. Consequently, I am in pain yet. I think I can give it a miss.'

Saunders sighed and got up, pattering down the corridor to the foyer. I heard the ringing stop, but I couldn't hear her murmuring conversation. After a time her steps returned and her face looked bright as she did. 'Good news.'

'Are you sure?' I wasn't willing to give an inch.

'Van der Peer.' I cursed involuntarily, regretting my pig-headedness. I hated to miss the chance to exchange salty words with her. 'She says we were right. Well, she said a lot of unrepeatable things first, but there's a kind of slow-acting sedative or muscle-relaxer drug inside the fake Viagra. Like alcohol, stimulates first then depresses.'

'I don't get it.'

'Suggestibility.' She sighed at my obtuseness. 'You know the remorse of the hangover? It's like that. So people are more likely to be influenced during the sort of hangover period after using the stimulant part.'

'So—?'

Saunders glared at me. 'We're talking about some attempt at mind control important enough to knock off Dockmuir's wife.'

'Whoa!' I held up my hands as if they would stop the flow of words. 'None of your wild five-bar-gate-and-over jumps there!'

'What?'

I started again with excessive and, I hoped, obvious patience. 'Dockmuir knocked off Peaches because she was going to leave him and take him for all she could. Just like he did with his previous wife.'

'No, that's not enough to knock off a wife for.'

'But the first one—'

'Yes, with care and subtlety and all manner of ambiguity as to her demise. Not gunning her down in front of witnesses.'

'With a good patsy for it,' I added with a grumble. 'Convenient that.'

'But hasty and messy and entirely questionable nonetheless.' Saunders gave me a very hard look. 'He had a contingency plan, ergo he was worried. She said the wrong thing and pow. No more Peaches.'

'I… suppose.' I threw myself back in my chair far too dramatically—anything but admit defeat.

'And now he's just trying to figure out if there's any truth to your psychic act—and whether he needs to do anything about it.' She gave me a meaningful look whose meaning did not entirely escape me.

'So I should shut the hell up already.' Easily done. I could shut up all day if need be. I began to plan my days out in silent bliss with no one living or dead prevailing upon me to speak. It would doubtless take a good bit of fairy dust, but if the job needed doing, I could get it done.

'We should see if there are any points of intersection between the locations mentioned by all these folks,' Saunders continued, obviously oblivious to the fine fantasy of withdrawal that I had constructed. 'Maybe we can pinpoint the warren from that. Do you have a map we could use?'

'A map?'

Jinx broke in to shake his head toward the library, as if I had suddenly forgot about its existence. He threw down his tea towel, ready to lead the expedition forth. I'd better nip that in the bud or he would want to be part of everything here.

And I wasn't sure how that would go.

'We got a few in the library I suspect, as Jinxy means to say. They may not all be from the current century though. Granddad wasn't fond of the newfangled. Very old hat.'

Jinx snorted. He had got very opinionated while I wasn't looking. Serves me right to get all injured and whatnot. 'The river's more or less in the same place. That's all right, Jinxy. We can find them on our own.' I led the way to the library, my nose only slightly out of joint.

The room exhaled a mild rebuke for its neglect as I opened

the door. A fine coating of dust about the place made my hand reach into my pocket for a refill but feeling Saunders' eyes upon me I lifted it out once more as if it had merely strayed there accidentally.

'Quite the collection,' she said, stopping to examine a barrister's case of thin leather-bound volumes.

'If you like that sort of thing,' I said, trying to hide a smile. Wait until she saw they were just pornographic novels. I tried to get my bearings for the rest of the room. It had been some years since I stepped in here. You could still smell the old man's pipe.

Saunders laughed as she lifted the glass door. 'My French is a bit rusty, but I think I get the gist.' She opened one of the books and smiled wider. 'Is that even physically possible? Oh, wait, there's two men there. I didn't see the one behind her.' She looked over at me. 'Can't believe you've neglected these for so long. Cobwebs on that part of your life, eh?'

'I don't know what you mean.' I concentrated on rummaging through the long drawer of the desk where I was pretty sure there were some maps of some kind, hopefully from a neighbouring century. Damn that woman, any other would have been blushing.

'If nothing else, this kind of vintage smut is worth quite a lot.'

I ignored her. 'Here's a map we can use.' It looked to date from about 1958 but was a handy size.

'Really, that's the most recent you have?' Saunders had her finger marking her place in the book, as if she intended to continue reading it. I had a funny feeling in my stomach but I didn't want her to think the wrong thing about it.

'It'll do to get a lay of the land. Let's go.'

'Why don't we just look at it here?'

'The light's all wrong. And it's so dusty.' I sneezed for emphasis.

'I thought you liked it dusty.'

'You're going to separate the binding if you keep your finger in there.'

Saunders grinned in a way that reminded me of the first

day we met. This did not seem optimal as she had had the upper hand of things then. 'Funny you should put it that way, seeing as how this picture was posed.'

'C'mon, let's go.'

'Are you blushing?'

I said nothing and headed back to the kitchen with the map, listening to hear if her steps were following me. They were, but I didn't want to look back because I knew she would still have that damn book with her. I spread the map out on the kitchen table and made a show of examining the surface of it. 'So what have we got for locations so far?'

Saunders set the book down on the edge of the table and gathered up her notes. I was hoping Jinx didn't take a gander at the title of the tome, not that I was sure he could read French—you just never knew with him. But he didn't need to get ideas, too. One of them with ideas was bad enough.

We pored through the scribbly notes in Saunders' mad hand and started marking sites on the map with condiments and magnets from the refrigerator. A pattern began to emerge, sure enough. There was a concentration of markers just past Tower Bridge. I would have put my money on Canary Wharf but maybe I had misunderstood the remark.

'You suppose Dockmuir's got some land down that way?'

I shrugged. 'I suppose we could look through leases or sales for the last few decades of whatnot. Sounds like your kind of thing.' I didn't sit back with my hands folded behind my head, but it was tempting to do so. And I did need some dusting for sure. I was losing my sparkle.

Saunders looked at me. 'We could shortcut the process.'

'How?'

She raised one of those dangerous eyebrows at me. 'Peaches.'

'Peaches!' I frowned.

'Can't you call her? Isn't she usually hanging about?'

With a bit of a shock I realised just how strange it was that she hadn't been around today, which was a bit unusual. Maybe because we had been out? I didn't want to think about other reasons. It was right that Peaches should pass over eventually, but I had grown accustomed to her face. And that smart mouth. 'Right.'

Saunders stared at me expectantly, which of course made it so much easier. It had been so long since I had tried to do anything like this. I had allowed people to come to me—well, lately anyway. I hadn't bid anyone come to me since—

Well, a very long time.

I suppressed the image of the young boy ever at my elbow, whose face threatened to swim into my vision. I closed my eyes, as if that would help or even make the slightest difference.

'Do you need to go to the other room?' Saunders and Jinx both stared at me, the former with something that had begun to approach impatience.

I sighed. 'Peaches, you out there? Yo, Peaches. Woman, you hear me?'

Silence. Well, not quite silence. The old clock ticked on. Out in the street rain fell. Again. My stomach gurgled. I reached for my pocket and found nothing. Time to replenish.

'Peaches?'

'I'm here!' And all at once she was and the look on her face was impossible to describe—a wild mix of happiness, fear, confusion, I guess, and maybe another half dozen emotions as well. 'I couldn't remember where I was... where I was going...' She wrapped a scarlet tipped set of claws around my wrist. 'I didn't... didn't...'

'Ouch,' I said as gently as I could, seeking to pry her nails off my arm.

'Sorry, but I really didn't know...' Her voice trailed off. 'I'm... dead.'

'I thought we had reconciled ourselves to that already, Peaches,' I said as gently as I could.

'Yeah, but, no, but yeah—I don't want to be!' Her wail made me wince.

'Then we need to nail the bastard who did this to you,' I said, trying to pat her insubstantial form without success.

'It won't be bring me back,' she pouted, sounding more like her old self.

103

'Well, maybe the shock will kill him and you can kick his arse from here to eternity.' It sounded like a great idea.

'Yeah, I might like that.' Peaches sniffled. I wondered if I ought to offer her a handkerchief. It likely wouldn't help much.

'Tell her about the map,' Saunders urged. Apparently her one-sided experience of the conversation did nor render it riveting.

'Peaches, you got any idea if Dockmuir owns property around this area?'

'Yeah, loads.' She bent over the map. 'This, this, this…' My heart sank and I sighed which Saunders heard.

'Loads,' I translated for her.

'This,' Peaches said, a red dagger poking at what looked like open space on the map. 'This is it.'

'It?'

'Where the rabbit is.'

'The warren you mean?' I gaped at her. 'Really? There's nothing there.'

'What?' Saunders said, leaning over, straining to see what Peaches was doing and inadvertently running an arm through her.

'How ancient is this map?' Peaches said with a snort. 'There's a big old building here. Slick, new—offices, meeting places. He don't own that, but it's under it.'

'Under?' I looked up at her puzzled.

'Yeah, like a rabbit hole. And a lot of people have disappeared down it.' Her face looked surprisingly grim. 'I saw a glimpse of something, when I started poking around. You know, trying to make sure I could milk him, right?'

'Right…'

'There's a huge flow of money through the white rabbit. Money they have to disguise somehow.'

'How?'

'I dunno! Do I look like an accountant?' Peaches regarded me with one fist on her hip.

'What?!' Saunders could no longer contain herself. 'What is she telling you?'

'There's a building—'

'A business centre.'

'All right, a business centre, here, and the warren is under that. And it's generating a lot of money. Money they have to hide.'

'How?' Saunders stared at the map with her laser eyes, trying to see through the non-existent building right to its hidden lower secrets.

'Do you know Peaches?'

She shook her head. 'That's why I wanted to talk to the previous missus. I figured she might give me a hint on what it was and how I could use it to fleece him. The bastard.'

'We need to go there,' Saunders said with what was surely reckless disregard for our health.

'Oi, that's how Peaches got shot.'

'Well, not precisely—'

'Close enough!' I stared at Saunders. Reporters! 'Poking her little nose into that place and its finances. I don't want to be shot.'

'I could use the company,' Peaches said with a admirable dryness.

I shot her a look. 'You're company enough right now.'

'We don't need to *do* anything,' Saunders hastened to add. 'But we should check it out, see the lay of the land.'

'We got a map.'

'The current lay of the land,' she insisted, poking the poor old paper for emphasis. 'See what we can see. We don't have to go up close to it, just see what we can see.'

'Maybe you should go,' I said, a soul without an ounce of chivalry. 'You could take Jinx.' Jinx stood up at once, eager to leave. The shine of sweat on his brow gave him away. I began to see what it was that had got him all jumped up of late. Next thing you knew, he'd be picking posies from the neighbour's garden and smoothing down his hair with a comb. What was left of it anyway.

'We need you to see what's hanging around the place in, ah, other ways. See if any of the recently deceased are limbo-ing around the joint.' Saunders could be so convincing when she wanted to be. 'You need to get this sorted before your life is a shambles.'

'My life is a shambles already. I like it that way.' Definitely time for some dust. I got up with some awkward stiffness as Peaches settled herself on the table's edge.

'It will get worse,' Saunders said, her voice ominous with doom, which I hoped to ignore.

'Let it.'

'Haven't you wondered why the tabs have left you alone? Billionaire trophy wife bumped off by cheap fake psychic—'

'Cheap!'

'—that theme should be screaming from the headlines daily, not buried in the back pages. But it's Dockmuir's rags that set the pace and they're all schtum.'

'Schtum!' I made my face into an expression of horrified shock. At least I wanted to believe it was. 'What are you, a gangster now? Schtum!' But she had a point. In my gratitude for the peace in which they'd left me, I'd never considered just how unbelievable that quiet was—and what ominousness it portended for little old me.

'I'll just need to pop to my room for a refresher.' That was non-negotiable. It certainly made the tube journey—if not bearable, then at least slightly more entertaining. People's faces grew softer and if the colours ran a little at first, though really it only enhanced what was normally a soul-sucking experience of sardine proportions. There was a pack of American students buzzing like wires from their first ever Shakespeare play, a father and daughter talking about ponies with great seriousness, and a pair of young German backpackers reading aloud from a book of lyrics with a garish orange cover.

'Was bedeutet 'mithering'?' the young woman said, wrinkling her nose with annoyance. 'K'nichts das sein.'

Her pal shrugged, looking impatient to get somewhere else. His skin seemed to be slipping off the bones of his face or maybe I had had too much dust. Nevertheless I was going to enjoy it while it lasted, and did.

Jinx sat silent as ever, his whole being attuned to Saunders who remained oblivious to it, sunk in a funk of irritation with me. If only she partook, she would understand. There is a sublime joy to life when you're just that bare inch off the ground, as if you'd come back from the fae having eaten something forbidden, never to touch the ground of your homeland again. There's a complete freedom in belonging nowhere.

We switched over at Bank, amidst unmitigated chaos. I found the bright colours of the adverts in the corridor fascinating, so Saunders had to drag me bodily along at times when I couldn't help but get distracted. There are times when blue looks so beautiful I just want to eat it.

By the time we got to Tower Hill I had settled down to a vague grin and a pervasive feeling of bonhomie for the world at large, which even the ravening crowds of bleating tourists about the station could not entirely quell. We slipped out onto the streets at last and made our way toward the intended site along East Smithfield.

We kept to the trees lining the dock side of the street. It all looked very business-like around there. People in suits scurried around, disappearing into the shiny façades of the various buildings. Nothing the least bit interesting around whatsoever.

Until we got near the warren.

Saunders didn't even have to remind me where it was. You'd have to be entirely dense not to notice. Judging by the oblivious characters around us, it was possible. My veins sang with dust and they caught the hum of it like an amplifier catching a buzzing guitar string.

I finally had to stop. Saunders wheeled around on the pavement. 'What?'

I shook my head. 'I'm not going anywhere near that place just now. Maybe later I could, but I don't know.'

'So there's… something there?' She looked back over her shoulder at the site.

'Something? Yeah, there's a lot of something there.' I shook my head while Jinxy looked concerned. Or was it puzzled? Hard to tell. 'I can't even tell what.'

'Is it bad?' Saunders suddenly looked uncomfortable.

'I—I don't really know.' I tried to separate the shivers of revulsion that coursed through my skin from the signals they were offering my grey cells. 'There's… like… a wall of sound.' I quashed the Phil Spector joke that wanted to rise to my lips.

'Some kind of protection?' Saunders frowned.

'I think. Maybe some. But the other sound. Sounds. Wailing. Lots and lots of wailing.' I shuddered. 'Can we get a little further away?'

The sound had begun to unsettle me, robbing all the glowing good feeling that had suffused my being only minutes before. I felt a kind of terror trying to work its tendrils into me, and it was making good headway. We cut between some of the sprawling business palaces to the dock of little pleasure boats and sat down to watch the river's flow.

That calmed me a little. Love that dirty water. It took all the flotsam and jetsam of this dirty old town and if it didn't wash it clean, it at least carried it away for a while.

'So any idea what it was? Giving you the fear?'

I shook my head. 'There's something very wrong in there.'

'What was it like?'

I stared at the lapping water. 'It was like hearing people die horribly. And slowly.' I looked up at her. 'You couldn't feel anything?'

She shrugged. 'Sorry.'

'Don't be. It was awful.'

'Could any of it be due to your, ah, intake?'

I snorted. 'I was feeling great until we got near that place and then it was all turned around at once. Horrible. It's the only word for it. Suffering.' My chest ached with it. What could do such a thing?

'We have to know more,' Saunders said, her words gentle though insistent.

'Not me.' I shook my head. 'You and Jinxy go see what you can see. I'm not going back there without a full suit of armour and earplugs.' The more I thought about it, the more it gave me the fear. Maybe some of the paranoia came from the dust, but I didn't think so. I had been cruising along so mellow. I felt as if a cold wind had worked under my clothes and got in my veins.

'Well, maybe we should go take a look at least,' Saunders said giving a quick nod to Jinx who looked ready to follow her across ice floes to the Antarctic. 'We may not see anything but at least we can see what we can see.'

'Yeah,' I said absently, trying to get a hold on my gibbering thoughts. The rising sense of panic seemed unaccountable. I knew I had heard an uncanny sound of suffering, but I should be able to shake it off. We all see terrible things that we have to force ourselves to forget somehow or we would spend all our time baying at the moon.

Well, I would.

I watched Saunders and Jinx walk away, then turned back to the river. There was only one: she had soothed countless agitated souls across the millennia. The sea refuses no river, the river refuses no pain. I let the waters take mine. That's the power of the river. Stilling the horrible echo of those voices with its ceaseless flow. Were they even voices? Maybe I had misinterpreted.

'All the waters flow by here, all the waters of the world.' A young woman in a cheap business suit sat awkwardly down on the bench next to me. I noticed I could see through her to the slats.

'Was this the first river? Can there be a first river?'

'Everything has to start somewhere.' She looked at me, a far away gaze in her eyes. 'And end. Everything has to end as well.'

'Did you end here?' Not meaning to pry you understand, but it was a nice distraction from what had been in my head before that and we were here for information after all.

'End? I haven't ended.' She looked at me confused. Her bloodshot eyes blinked at me uncertainly.

I didn't want to traumatise the woman. 'Are you tied to this spot?' A more polite way to proceed with the dead. Never ask about how they died unless they bring it up themselves first. I did know a thing or two, when I chose to remember it.

'Yes, here. I've been here a while.' Her brow furrowed as she tried to unspool the mystery of her time.

'Do you work around here?' It was a guess based on her clothing.

'No, a conference... I was at a conference. There was the screaming,' she glanced up at me, tears suddenly falling down her cheek. 'It was unbearable. I found I couldn't hear anything else. I ran out at the break and I—I—I knew I couldn't go back.'

'So you came here?'

She looked up at me, blinking. 'Did you hear them?'

'Yes.'

'What is it?' She grabbed my arm. Insubstantial though it was, I could feel the terror in its grip.

'I don't know,' I said truthfully enough. 'But we're trying to find out.'

'The rabbit.' She stared down at her shoes again. 'The rabbit is there.'

'Is it?' I sat very still, afraid to make any movement that might frighten her off. Something tangible would be nice. 'Have you seen it?'

'No, just the adverts.'

It was my turn to blink. 'Adverts?'

'You haven't seen them? They're everywhere. Like Scientologists. But they don't do personality tests. I've done the rounds on most. Guess you'd call me a seeker.'

I might call her a few other things, too, but who was I to judge. 'So you saw the adverts and then went to the warren?'

'No, never made it there. Though I suppose that's why I volunteered for the conference. I knew it was down... stairs... no stairs.' She looked up at me then over at the river. 'The water.'

'The river?'

'No,' she paused. 'Who are you again?'

'Just a guy on a bench. You were telling me about the rabbit.'

'The rabbit?'

See what I mean about the dead? They get caught in sort

of loops of habit that repeat. You can't always get something out of them. She might cross over just because she finally had someone to talk to—or she might be here for decades. I looked at her suit more carefully. It was cheap material, but I couldn't really say if it were recent or not.

So much for my keen fashion sense.

'The rabbit, you were interested in seeing the rabbit.'

She shook her head. 'Not seeing it, seeing about it. I just wanted to be among people who understood...'

'Understood what?' I had begun to get impatient, hoping that Saunders and Jinx would return, that I wouldn't have to keep going round in circles with this woman. I was tired. My head pounded, but I didn't want to take more dust. Something mellower, something to make me forgetful. Something that could take me all the way back to a time when the pain of daily life didn't outweigh its joys.

When would that be? When I was five years old, or six? Surely no more than eight. Once you get to puberty you're pretty much fucked.

'What it was I lost,' the woman said, reminding me there was a conversation going on around here, though I had lost the thread to it all together because I realised what I really wanted was a pint and I wanted to be drinking it in Marinova's pub with her telling me it would all be all right, which she never did but maybe just this once I could convince her it was a medical necessity, a mercy killing or whatever, and her smooth contralto could soothe away the echo of those terrifying yowls of pain and I would be once more forgetful and at peace with the world, all of them.

'I lost my way,' the woman said, standing uncertainly, her eyes on the river.

'We all do from time to time,' I assured her, thinking of Marinova's raven tresses and a nice pint of stout pulled the right way.

'I can't go back there,' the woman said with a stifled sob, then ran and jumped into the water. I jumped to my feet and then remembered it was already too late and collapsed back on the bench and put my head in my hands.

It was just too much—with or without dust, I was not capable of this much borrowed sorrow. Saunders would berate me, but I had to get far from this place. I hopped up and started off on my jerky walk, feeling unaccountably stiff from sitting just a short while.

And ran into Saunders and Jinx by the next turning. 'Where are you going?'

'Away from here,' I muttered not even slowing my steps.

She stared after me then reluctantly followed, Jinxy trailing behind her. 'What is it? What happened?'

'Doubtless nothing as far as you could tell,' I said, tired of her eternal doubt and derision. 'Nothing you could feel.'

'Look, I can't help it if—'

I whirled around. 'Don't, just don't. I'm in no mood to withstand your sneering or your carping or your inability to see the world around you.' I hunched my shoulders and turned back on my way.

'Look, just because I don't understand or experience things the way you do—'

I stopped. I didn't turn. There was something in me that had been fighting its way up for a while. I didn't think I could make her understand, though I was beginning—just beginning, mind you—to comprehend what we were up against.

And I didn't like it.

To be entirely truthful, it scared the fuck out of me and there wasn't much fuck left in me to scare. 'It's a drug.'

'What?' Saunders stood beside me now, doubt and worry fighting for space on her kisser.

'It's the drug of the century—this century for sure, but maybe every century.'

'I don't know what—'

'Fear.' I said it quiet like at first, but I knew as I said it I was right. 'It's fear. Fear that the world is ending. Fear that the tsunami has your name on it, or that the guy you met in the pub is really the new Yorkshire Ripper or that while you drink your tea at work a madman will be gunning down your children at school or thugs breaking into your mum's home, raping her and stealing your granddad's silver pocket watch.

Fear that no one ever loved you or ever could and that deep down inside you deserve to be the last person left on a trembling and poisoned planet when everyone else has said adios and thanks for all the fish.'

'But how—' Saunders stared at me, looking uncomfortable, though whether it was what I said or how mad I sounded, I couldn't tell.

'They're making a factory for it,' I said, hastily blinking away something in my eye. 'It's all there, that's what that place is. That's what his whole empire is built upon.'

'Dockmuir?'

Irrational anger seized me. It wasn't Saunders' fault that she was deaf, dumb and blind to it all. But I hated so much always being alone in the knowledge of what was really out there. It made me want to hit her or hit something or someone else. Maybe Jinxy. He could take it. 'Yes, Dockmuir. The murdering mogul. The owner of that atrocity factory. The one who's going to want me and you dead with a lot of suffering beforehand just to be sure we can add something to the pot.'

Now, there was a thought I didn't want to have. Saunders' eyes got even bigger. God, what a glorious face she had. If there were world enough and time enough—but I could feel the shudders wanting to come upon me again. I desperately needed something to take away this shaky mantle of dread. A golden grail of Guinness lit the path to hope. There had to be a pub around here somewhere.

'C'mon,' I grabbed her arm and Jinxy trotted along behind us like an obedient pooch. I steered us toward the touristy area, sure we'd find some kind of watering hole even if it pullulated with the hoi polloi. As long as it had the nectar of the old land, I could live with that.

We found a spot, far from ideal (in fact fairly wretched and soulless and packed to the gills), but they had Guinness and they had Jameson and after the gold and the black and a second round ordered, I began to feel a mite calmer, almost human again.

Saunders sipped her first pint and waited with reasonable

patience. Well, more reasonable than I would have been. 'Okay, I know I sounded like a madman,' I began.

'Not unusual that,' Saunders said, but she actually smiled when she said it. Her smiles were worth a long walk through the land of the muttering coach-packaged riders.

'Enough you. I don't mean to sound like doom and gloom, and I know you can't hear what I hear or see what I see.' I paused for some Irish courage, nodded to Jinx who was enjoying his pint and doubtless the proximity to his *lady love*. 'But there's a horror in that building that I can't comprehend—or bear—and I think it has a lot to do with a whole lot of dead people, *and* you might better want to think just how much we should tangle with this Dockmuir fella because it's even worse than we thought.'

Saunders' eyes widened at this longer than usual and far more impassioned speech from me. 'What did you hear?'

I shuddered. It was involuntary, but a bat's squeak of terror needled in, like the spearhead of a terror that threatened to fill my ears until I shut it out at once, a series of steel doors crashing down like a Bond villain's secret lair closing behind Jimbo and damning him to some utterly ridiculous fate. 'It's beyond words.'

'Try. I have to understand.'

'No,' I said downing the heavenly elixir. 'You don't.'

She stared at me over her Guinness. I could hear the wheels turning nonetheless. I suppose curiosity was natural and all that, but I didn't want to satisfy it. However much Pandora might have wanted to open the box, the horrible things inside it weren't worth the risk. And I had no hope to offer at the bottom of the trunk. Nothing I heard in that warren suggested hope.

All I wanted was to render myself deaf, especially to the deceased among us, one of whom stood behind the bar glowering at the chattering crowds, as if to burn them with some kind of laser vision.

What a way to spend eternity!

'But we need to figure out a way to stop him.' Saunders gave her best we-gotta-save-the-world pleading face.

'Not there, somewhere else.' *At a great distance*, I assured myself. 'I don't want to be anywhere near that place.'

'I can go back and reconnoitre,' Saunders said too easily.

'Don't. At least not yet,' I added before she got the set look to her face. Jinxy watched us both as if it were Wimbledon, his empty pint glass before him.

'Why not?'

I sighed. 'What did you see?'

Saunders shrugged. 'A conference centre. They were scanning badges so we couldn't really go in, but it looked all ship-shape from the outside.'

'Maintaining the façade, I suppose.'

'We need to get inside.'

'Not without knowing a lot more.' Easier to delay than to deny. 'I met someone.'

'Someone?'

'Someone of the ethereal persuasion.'

'You mean a spook?'

'There's no call to be rude.' As if it ever stopped me. 'But she had a few titbits of information that shed a light somewhat on the situation, at least as far as how they stock the shelves.'

'Stock the shelves?' She gaped at me a moment, but then twigged what I was getting at. 'Find victims for the atrocity factory?'

'Bingo.'

'And?'

'And what?'

'How do they?'

I laughed and downed the last of my Guinness. 'They advertise, of course.'

Saunders raised one of those inimitable eyebrows conveying the equivalent of a warning shot over the bow. 'They advertise? "Victims needed; large scale fear-mongering project of indefinite scope. Must have computer skills." Like that?'

'It might work, you know.' I nodded to Jinxy who got up for another round, weaving his way through the crowd who seemed to part like an archduke's hair to let him past.

'You think?'

'Yeah, but that's not how they do it. Think! How do all the other ones do it?'

Saunders blinked. 'Other ones?'

'Cults!'

'Cults? The rabbit is a cult?' Her look of surprise quickly turned into one of cogitation.

'Yes, or at least pretends to look like one.' I had begun to realise it was a very cunning plan indeed, so cunning it could call itself Charley and no one would gainsay it. 'Draws people in, somehow turns them into, um, horrified corpses that no one misses.'

She squinted at me. 'How?'

'I don't know; it's a mystery.'

Saunders grimaced and took the pint that a reappearing Jinxy offered. 'So how come we've never heard of this cult?'

'Easy,' I said, reaching across to get the pint my employee left a little too far from my reach. We would have to have words and all things considered, those words would all be coming from me. 'When do we hear about cults?'

'Usually when they've massacred each other or any large group of people. Or control Hollywood.'

'Right! Drink the Kool-Aid, meet your alien overlords in matching tie and handkerchiefs, or be the last man standing in some Texas compound.'

'Why are they always Texas and why compounds?' Saunders said idly, staring of into the crowd.

'What else is there in Texas?'

'I was in Houston once. There were nice restaurants.'

'Did you stay?'

'No.'

'Anyway—'

'Yes, anyway—what does all this mean?'

'What if you were a quiet cult, that didn't want all that media attention? You attract people steadily without much fuss. Keep it all on the 'down low' as they say.'

'That's not what that phrase means.'

'Don't be pedantic.'

'But why keep it so quiet? Wouldn't they get more people if they made a bigger noise? You can't take over the world without an army of some kind.'

'What if you're not trying to take over the world, just to power some kind of... engine.'

'Engine?'

'Well, something. What does a factory make? You want a steady stream, but you don't want anyone to ask what you're building in there.'

She gave me that patented Saunders appraisal. 'So we need to do research? Or rather, I need to do research.'

'I expect so.' That was me off the hook for a while then. How ever would I fill my time?

'Well, drink up and let's roll.'

'I love it when you talk like a gangster.' I wish I could describe the exasperated look she gave me just then, but words fail me. For some reason it buoyed my sinking spirits more than the booze. Dutifully I drank the rest of my pint off and Jinx did the same, finishing hers as well when she offered it to him. Don't think I didn't notice that.

We trooped together to the tube station and my thoughts, while not yet coherent, were a good deal more settled than they had been. Somehow the touristy throngs were just enough to distract me from my shaky thoughts and naturally the fine elixirs of the ancient land did their best to soothe my troubled spirit.

When I heard a bird song every Londoner knows, my mind leapt into action. This was not a statement I could make often, especially after a couple of pints, but somehow the cry of 'G'issue!' made the spark leap the gap and fire the old incandescent. A genuine idea! I gave the fellow selling the mags a pound and took the much-wrinkled copy he had on offer. A gormless pop star looked serious on the cover.

Once we were seated on the train I began to flip through *The Big Issue*, starting with the back. If there was going to be one, I knew it would be somewhere in those pages. Sure enough, I spotted the outline of a rabbit. It was a small enough advert, but the text was striking—and simple.

We can show you the way, was all it said. There was a telephone number, too. I showed it to Saunders.

'Shall I call them?' She pulled out her wee mobile.

I felt a rush of panic. 'Should you?'

'No harm in it, is there? We can at least see what they say and how they answer.'

I nodded at the little machine in her hand. 'They can't track you from that thing, can they?'

Saunders blinked at me. 'The little man inside here runs around too quickly to be tagged by their little man.'

'I'm not an idiot and I resent the fact that you think I am completely technologically illiterate.' I sniffed in high dudgeon, or at least mid-level dudgeon. 'I know you can record phone numbers of people who call.'

'They could record it but that's of limited use. They can phone me back, I can ignore it as I do all numbers I don't know. You see, the advantage of these little gadgets is that you can see who is calling you without actually answering.'

I ignored her sarcasm. I liked my old Bakelite. It was sturdy and beautiful and if it came down to it, a good weapon in hand-to-hand combat. Never mind that it might be one of the first telephones ever to be used in Britain. 'Nonetheless, they don't need to have information about you.'

She sighed. 'Do you know the unlikelihood of finding a working payphone in the city?'

Good point. Most telephone boxes were missing the actually machinery in question, serving instead as the backdrop for any number of genteel calling cards for the rumpy-bumpy trade. And quite a variety there was, too. They could entertain me for hours. 'I suppose that's true.'

We had to wait until we were up top again anyway in order for her to get a signal, so we got out at the Oval and made our way to the Hanover for a pint in a quiet corner. That was my argument, of course. 'It only makes sense. Too much noise from the traffic on the street.'

'Yeah, because a pub is never noisy,' Saunders said with her usual sardonic tone as Jinx brought the drinks.

'This one's quiet at the moment.' I sipped my black dream

and wished I had a little more in my pocket to enhance the experience. I had a bad feeling about this phone call business. 'Maybe we should make someone else call.'

'It's just a phone call. Just to see what they say.'

Saunders' tone soothed but I wasn't entirely placated. 'What if they ask something tricky, like 'Who are you?''

'I might get at least seventy-five per cent on that,' Saunders said before hastily sipping her pint to hide a smile. Jinxy shook with silent mirth, but I scowled at her. 'Seriously, it's just a phone call. We had more at risk visiting their headquarters today.'

I blinked at her. 'Why?'

'Security cameras,' she said, narrowing her gaze at me. Even Jinx shook his head at me. What a dolt. 'With luck they aren't going to go looking through the tedious amount of footage accumulated daily unless they have a reason to do so, but let's not give them a reason to do so.'

'Like being implicated in murder,' I grumbled.

'We have the advantage of them,' Saunders insisted. 'It looks to be a large enough organisation, *and* part of an even larger one—if it's all Dockmuir's, it's an enormous one spread across numerous countries. So they would have trouble finding something they were actually looking for—and they would really have to be looking in order to find us.'

Sure, it sounded like logic, but that didn't mean I had to find it compelling. 'I... suppose.'

'Drugs are making you paranoid.'

'Who says?' I muttered into my pint. 'All right, then. Call and see what they say.'

'My guess is a kindly-voiced phone bank.'

'Like the Samaritans.'

'Exactly. They want to lure you in, give you hope and then somehow steal your soul or whatever it is they do.'

'Not like the Samaritans. I think.' I did my best to look unconcerned but my heart was in my mouth while she called. I knew it was absurd to fear I'd hear those screams down the line or that they'd somehow suck Saunders through the ether, but I couldn't help being afraid of it all the same.

She tapped the number into the phone. The little rabbit outline in the advert took on a cast of menace for me as we waited, as if it might sprout fangs and leap off the page to attack. I wouldn't put it past that reprehensible man.

Who might have us tailed even now, I realised. A sudden bouquet of sweat jumped to my brow. With care I looked around the pub at the quick and the dead, but no one seemed to be paying us the slightest notice—not that that meant anything, I supposed.

'Yes, hello.' Saunders said into the tiny phone. 'Is this the white rabbit?'

An hysterical part of my brain wanted to imagine that the March Hare was on the other end of the line and expecting to chat with the Mad Hatter. A few more handfuls of dust and I could fit the job description. I really itched to be home and indulging. I needed a break from all this stress and unaccustomed labour. The echoes of the screams still scratched the inside of my skull and I longed to soothe that all away with a spell of forgetting.

'I don't know,' Saunders said warily, 'I was just wondering what you were about. I saw you in a magazine.'

It's always hard listening to one side of a conversation. I tried to get clues from her face, but I got distracted noticing details about it I hadn't made note of before. She had a scar on her cheek that looked like teeth marks. I wondered who would have been mad enough to bite her in the face that hard, then realised it was probably a pet, a dog maybe.

I hoped.

The idea of someone hurting her gave me a funny feeling in my chest. I looked over at Jinxy whose face betrayed only a simple adoration of the woman. I both envied his directness and despised it. What right had he?

What right had I? I, who had nothing, I who was—

'Come by?' Saunders said, the two words filled with doubt and a little bit of dangerous eagerness. 'Well, I don't know.'

I shook my head at her but she pointedly ignored me, listening intently to the voice on the line. I wondered briefly if I should do something more, if I could listen to the conversation or if the ether of the telephone line had a different life altogether, more so because there was no physical line—and wondered why it had never occurred to me to see how far the ability could go.

'I suppose I could,' Saunders said with reluctance. She grabbed a pencil from her bag and scribbled something on the edge of the beer mat. An address, it appeared to be. At last she rang off and looked up at the two of us staring at her.

Awkward moments always seem to last longer than they do.

'The conference centre must not be the first line of attack,' she said finally, tapping the beer mat. 'They have an office in Soho that seems to be the welcome centre or whatever.'

'Probably a front for a nude ladies dancing club,' I said because I didn't know what else to say.

'It's a way in,' she said, unfazed by my suggestion or else ignoring it all together. 'We can figure out what they're up to.'

'You're not going?'

She blinked at me. 'Of course I am.'

'Look, this is dangerous—'

'All of this is dangerous!' She stared at me as if I were the crazy one, but she kept her voice low enough that only I could hear. 'Dockmuir wants us out of the picture one way or another. If he doesn't think we're doing so of our own accord, he will make sure we are. A man who guns down his own wife isn't going to worry too much about gunning down a couple of people who mean nothing to him—as soon as he's sure they haven't got anything he needs.'

Her logic was unassailable, which made it all the more galling. 'When are you supposed to go?'

The next morning Saunders and I made our way to Soho. I manoeuvered things so that Jinx had a few tasks to keep him busy. It was small of me, I suppose, but I had the reasoning of security and caution on my side. After all, if you were going to remember any one of us, it was either Saunders' striking looks or the big lummox. I could pretty much count on invisibility, as I had no redeeming characteristics in my visage and a generally slovenly appearance that invited the eye to pass over without remark.

I also had a pocket full of dust, which improved my mood considerably. I wanted to be reasonably calm for the encounter, even if most of my work consisted of casing the joint, watching for people going in and out, and standing by in case Saunders needed me.

'It won't be anything at all,' she told me as we parted ways at the door of the little café around the corner where we agreed I would wait. 'Just a first step. They won't want to overwhelm a possible new recruit.'

'I suppose.'

'We just want information.' She looked at me with some hint of an appeal. For what? Agreement? Acquiescence? Approval?

'Information? You won't get it.'

A sunny smile then. 'By hook or by crook we will.' She flounced off to make her appointment and I ordered a cuppa and something sweet and tried to ignore the crowds. I had called in vain for Peaches the night before. That worried me. The rest of the insubstantial, however, had no trouble making their presence known.

'I hate Mondays,' a shimmery young person of indeterminate gender said from across the table.

'It's Thursday,' I said with a perfunctory crossness, wincing as I sipped from the giant mug.

'Then I'm late!' The diaphanous figure abruptly exited the café, leaving me to mutter that he or she was even later than they thought. That's the thing about Soho: it's full of spooks.

Or whatever it was I should be calling them, I thought, mindful of Peaches' words. I was missing the gal. Despite shout outs I couldn't find her at all last night and that was a bit worrying considering what her almost-ex had got himself up to these days. The idea that he could have sucked her into that horrifying void while I was near it disturbed me even more. Say what you will about the coarseness of Ms

Dockmuir neé Weiner, she was a pistol and I wouldn't want to think of her suffering in that way.

I was glad I didn't have a watch as I would have been casting a glance at it every other minute while I waited, fingers drumming on the table next to the too big mug. There was, however, a large clock over the door and my gaze continually strayed over to it as if that might make the time pass more quickly.

It did not.

I watched the crowds of people on the pavement, some wandering, some purposeful. Here a young man clearly on a job interview; there a stunning looker disappearing into a real estate office—I assumed. With a name like Baskingstoke Developments, LLC it could be just about anything, and a woman that gorgeous—no way she was an estate agent. Probably a spy or something.

I was considering ordering another reservoir of tea when at last Saunders returned, her face aglow with the signs of success.

'All right?'

'All right.' She plopped herself down and slapped a big folder down on the table. It was plain white except for the black outline I now regarded with loathing: a running rabbit. Or leaping. Or is that only lords?

'How did it go?' I was almost afraid to ask; she looked so pleased.

'It was fine, fine,' Saunders looked around the café. 'Should we go somewhere quieter?'

And she could only see the living. 'Good idea.'

'All right. I know just the place.' She smiled again. We got up and I trotted after her eager steps, down Shaftesbury and then along Charing Cross. 'Here,' she said unexpectedly and we stepped into the library, which I'd forgotten all about. Saunders smiled at the librarians as we made our way to the back. I remembered this place now: the Chinese collection was housed here. That accounted for the particular population of ghosts here; libraries were always full of ghosts.

Fortunately, they were usually busy themselves and didn't bother anyone. Imagine having all that time to read.

Saunders put the folder on the table and whispered, 'It's all about recruitment, it is. A wonder of rhetoric.'

'As we guessed,' I said trying to sound suave and on top of things. What I really felt was a hollow sort of fear that I tried very hard not to give way to just then. 'I expect they don't immediately tell you about wanting to swallow your soul.'

'No, no, of course not,' she said as she flipped through the pages. 'It's all about being lost at the start, finding your way. But that gives way to the will to power. Interesting rhetoric. Reminds me of something…'

'Hitler Youth?'

She gave me a patented Saunders eyebrow-plus-mildly-sardonic-grin. Wrap it in a stripy box and you could sell them for top price at Selfridges. 'Sneer away, but it's a delicate sort of crafty writing, both persuasive and subtly aggrandising.'

'I don't see the point,' I grumbled, feeling out of my depths. Clearly Saunders was in hers, which made me feel oddly disconnected, as if I were sinking in quicksand while she ran along the stony path.

Christ on a crutch, not half getting full of the flowery rhetoric myself.

'The point,' she continued on without paying the slightest attention to my waffling mooning, 'is to lure in people on the edge and convince them not only is there a reason to live, but that reason is because the powerless can become very powerful and they're going to help you do it.'

'Like most cults, I suppose.'

'But also like secret societies. It's like a combination of the two.' She pointed to a colourful page of ribbons and plaques. 'People can advance with purpose, but they have to be in it to win it. Carrots dangled before them, but the stick isn't shown.' Saunders looked up, her thoughts clearly elsewhere. 'I wonder how far in they have to lure people before they can victimise them.'

'And what if they discover they have lives and families or

other people who will miss them?' There were bound to be some, surely.

'I wonder if they keep them on board, string them along.' Saunders flipped through more of the glossy pages, examining the shiny happy people smiling from them. 'After all, an organisation this big needs bureaucrats to run it.'

'The true horror.' I took the brochure reluctantly, as if it might somehow be contagious. 'Maybe they need a special kind of mind for their factory of screams. That's why Peaches ended up dead instead of screaming.'

She appeared to consider this, by which I mean she stared off into space, seemingly unaware of the ancient Chinese woman at her elbow, her back curved with age, a gleaming smile on her face as she murmured something to me that I could not understand, though the beatific expression suggested good will. Her hand rested a moment on my arm and then she moved on.

Despite myself, I felt a surge of hopefulness. It evaporated with Saunders' next words. 'I'm going to get recruited.'

'No. Bad idea. Not good.' I shook my head. 'In fact, I think that's incredibly stupid.'

'I'll be fine. We need information. It's a big organisation, huge in fact, I think.' Her face glowed with a look I knew all too well from my old working days: the hunt.

'We can find another way in.'

'You do know that the important part of secret organisation is that they remain, you know, *secret*.'

'Yes, but we don't have to know everything,' I said, knowing my words were falling far short of convincing. 'It's just too dangerous.'

'More dangerous than waiting around for Dockmuir to decide we're too much trouble to let live?'

I spluttered, 'You're going to make sure he decides we're too much trouble!' A shush came not from a librarian but from a pair of old men reading the dailies. Nonetheless I felt immediately chastened and more than that, I felt a growing sense of paranoia that had nothing to do with the dust coursing through my veins. 'You can't do this.'

'Watch me.' Saunders got up, handing me the brochures. 'You keep going through these. Figure out the buzz words, likely turns of phrase we need to watch for, any clues as to the way they work. The structure has to hold up the secret levels as well as the more visible ones.'

'No, this is crazy, you can't be serious about this,' I continued to hiss as I followed her out of the building into the street.

Saunders stopped on the pavement. The matinee crowds were beginning to make themselves known, buzzing excitedly about the new hit play, as the clouds began to lower over us. 'I know it's a risk, but we're going to have to take some risks if we want to find out anything about this White Rabbit business.'

'But they know you!'

Saunders shook her head. 'Dockmuir knows me. How much does the average CEO know about the running of his empire? A big fat nothing. Dockmuir's not the hands-on type. He's the belligerent shouter at sporting events, the lording it over them at grand dinners, hanging around polo matches sort. He won't be keeping up on the day to day running of the place.'

'I don't know. I've got a bad feeling about this…'

'You're just paranoid.' Saunders touched my arm and I experienced a strange feeling of déjà vu. 'I'll be back tonight. Don't worry.'

She turned and walked briskly away and, like any good heroine, didn't look back. I felt more bereft than I had in many a day, so I went to the Portrait Gallery to sneer at the powerful men looking smugly out from their canvases.

'You're all shite,' I muttered at the fifteenth earl of whatever gurning estate he was. A docent gave me a grim look of death. Well, stuff this for a laugh. I decided to go where the people understood me.

Across the street to Chandos for a pint I ventured and found a seat near the back door. It took a bit of effort to block out the incessant chatter of the throngs of people living and dead—why was it that actors and singers and such had to blather on so?—but I had to do some serious cogitating. I had found it a bit annoying what with all this running around, knees bent, dancing behaviour, that I hadn't had a chance to get properly dusted, but perhaps it was just as well.

What the hell was Saunders doing?!

I stared down into my pint as if its golden bubbles held the answer. They didn't. I felt an unfamiliar mix of worry and exasperation. My feet became so antsy that I knew I wouldn't be able to stay there long. I upended the pint and headed out onto the pavement to fight my way through the inevitable crowds, though I stayed on the St. Mark's side as long as possible.

Heading down into the tube I was already through the turnstiles before I thought, *where am I going?* Before I could answer that question, my feet lumbered me on my way and I knew where it was after all, though I didn't think it was a spectacularly good idea. Nonetheless I was outside the old station house before it seemed possible and that realisation stopped me in my tracks for sure. I couldn't really go in, but it took some doing to finally find a working payphone to call my former partner and took even more doing to get through to him. No one wanted to talk to me.

'You got anything? Otherwise leave me alone.'

'That's a fine way to talk to your former partner.' I sniffed as if wounded.

Coburn snorted. 'Emphasis on former.'

'I need to ask you something, but not like this.' I closed my eyes to shut out the cartoonish parade of scantily clad women plastered all over the interior of the box, promising to give me whatever I needed from their silicon lips and balloon-like breasts.

'Like what?' Coburn wasn't giving an inch, damn his rhinoceros carcass.

'Meet me at the café,' I wheedled, trying not to sound as desperate as I felt.

'No,' he said before I heard a click, but when I went there he appeared not too long after I did.

'Thanks for coming.'

Coburn sniffed. 'I'm only here for the caffeine.' The waitress, who looked ancient enough to have been big sister to the elder gods who slept under the oceans, had already brought a tray, remembering through the mists of time our orders of yesteryear with uncanny accuracy. I stared at the clouds in my coffee trying to bring a tune to mind and recalling the last time I had actually had coffee here. How much had changed irrevocably since that day.

'Like old times,' I said, feeling a sudden attack of shyness.

'You mean you're wasting my time?' His words were harsh but Coburn sipped his coffee as if he weren't necessarily in a hurry to get somewhere else.

I steeled myself to the task. 'I'm getting a little uneasy about this whole 'white rabbit' thing.'

'What whole 'white rabbit' thing? You've said nothing about that. Or have Dockmuir's goons dropped you on your head again?'

I ignored that. 'We've been looking into this cult thingee that Dockmuir's place seems to be connected to, at least one of his places.'

Coburn said nothing for a moment, just swirled his coffee until I thought I would scream with frustration but I kept a lid on it. 'There was always something dodgy about that man, beyond his self-aggrandising and empire-building.'

'This has got me spooked, especially since Saunders is playing guinea pig at present.'

Coburn actually looked up. 'That wise?'

'No,' I said with a scowl, 'It's not, but you try to tell that woman anything—' I shrugged.

To my surprise, Coburn laughed heartily and long, until his eyes were streaming with tears. I gaped at him. No idea what could set the man off. He was always thus. Enigmatic. He finally dabbed his cheeks almost daintily with his napkin and took another sip of coffee, continuing to grin at me.

'I don't see what's so funny.'

He shook again with mirth. 'I know.'

'I'm worried!'

He did his best to restore a look of concern. 'Tell me what you've discovered so far.'

I spelled out the workings of the place as far as we could tell, skating over the evidence supplied by the non-corporeals as much as possible. Coburn's eyebrows kept shooting up anyway, not so much to suggest disbelief as dismay—or so I hoped.

'I'll see what I can find out about disappearances in the area or any other kind of report that might suggest a link. I can have a word with our cult squad, see what they know.'

'They got a cult squad now?' I was impressed.

Coburn shrugged. 'Things have changed a lot since your time. We move with the times.'

'I wouldn't go that far.'

'You want help or not?'

'I am chastened and grateful.'

Good-bye ended up as awkward as hello had been. I felt weird about shaking hands or something. It seemed too formal for what we had been—and not formal enough for what we'd lost. Gone was our old easy way of yakking together. What had we done back then to say fare-thee-well? Clap each other on the shoulder in an oh-so-manly way? I didn't even recall. And Coburn was so prickly I wasn't about to try anything like that now.

'You take care,' I finally said, the words feeling less than successful.

'You be on your guard.' Coburn said, sizing me up with a look that said as much as if I had passed some kind of test and had begun the laborious journey toward forgiveness. 'And don't let that woman endanger herself too much.'

'That's my plan.' It had to be a bit of a stretch to call the vague shapes in my head a 'plan' but there was enough of an idea to make it believable. Well, enough for me. Likely that counted with no one else. Coburn's parting glance seemed to cast reasonable doubt upon my likely success, yet I tried to consider it a vote of confidence none the less. I was grasping at straws these days for sure.

I walked out of there with my steps, if not quite sprightly, at least lighter. I didn't even feel an urge for a sprinkle of dust just yet. Well, maybe just a small one. After all, I needed to occupy myself in some useful way until Saunders returned tonight.

Or maybe a useless way: I wasn't particular when you got right down to it. I let my feet take me where I was bound as once again I had no idea where that might be at the moment. I did my best not to worry about that scamp Saunders, but it became clear that not thinking about her ended up taking up a fairly expansive swath of my brain function. So I let my steps mind themselves. Funny how feet generally know where to take you as long as you give them their head, if that makes any sense. Not sure that it does, but it worked.

I found myself at the threshold of Marinova's establishment. The doors of the Silver Wheel opened at my touch as if beckoning me inside. I know, most pubs do that just as well but her doors always seemed to know my name and welcome the press of my hand upon them.

And there was the woman herself, a restorative sight at any time. 'I've come to demand your hand in marriage, my dear.' The place was empty save for a ragged looking case in the corner nursing a Jameson and Guinness combination, with a bright set of new choppers and a nasty scar across his cheek. I wasn't sure I wanted to know his story. Marinova drew an odd crowd.

I ought to know.

Marinova raised one dark eyebrow at my assertion. 'My hand? You'll have to talk to my father, you know.'

I sat down at the bar on the stool with one gammy leg and coughed from habit. 'Oh, then I'll pass on it for now. Never could abide the whiff of brimstone that followed him about.'

'You're in a rare mood,' the dark beauty said as she poured me out a generous helping of Lagavulin and set it before me.

I lifted the glass and looked into its chunky depths. I knew drinking up meant I accepted the need to pay—and it wasn't always folding money that she wanted. Worse, I had to ask a favour, I suddenly realised. That's what my tricksey feet were up to, damn them. I took a big mouthful of the golden nectar, which made my tongue want to dance. 'I find myself in the awkward position of not knowing things.'

'Things you would wish to know?' Marinova smiled, but crossed her arms.

'Things maybe I ought to know.' I could be stubborn, too.

'Maybe?'

'You can tell me if I ought to know or not,' I said, trying to be reasonable. 'You're good at obscure, smoke and mirrors sort of whatnot, eh? You can hide the truth right under my nose and have me running the long way around.'

Marinova had a speculative look in her eye that made me shiver a little inside, as if she were sorting out just how much I might be able to handle—which worried me a good bit, to be sure. 'Cards.'

It wasn't a question. She went over to the till and unlocked the drawer beneath it, opening it to pull out a small wooden box. I could feel my pulse quicken. It had been years since I had seen her cards.

As a practitioner of the arts—or more often, a faker of them—I had a fine selection of packs myself. Mostly ornate, colourful and shinily new to impress the punters who didn't find the crystal ball malarkey to their taste. My favourite set was a Bacchus tarot (go on, act surprised) featuring medieval woodcuts. The images were a bit clunky and it wasn't sleek or all that eye-catching, but they had a plainness that always delivered.

Marinova, on the other hand, had a pack of ordinary playing cards.

Well, when I say ordinary, they were ordinary and *old*. I often figured they might well have been the cards that famous Alice fell asleep over and had her dreams with—except of course I know Alice wasn't real, was she? I mean there was an Alice but she wasn't really *Alice* after all, right?

Now even I'm confused.

Marinova opened the box and drew out the cards. They were wrapped in a green lace handkerchief or scarf. It had embroidery of flowers and birds and bees and a few symbols I never quite recognised.

'Did you embroider that?' I asked with honest curiosity.

She shook her head. 'My grandmother. They were her cards.' Smoothing the folds of the fabric out, Marinova traced the lines of ivy with affection.

'Her name wasn't Alice, was it?'

She laughed and picked up the pack. The box that held them was frayed at the edges and ready to fall apart. The curiously ornate lettering and plain look of 19th century printing fixed its age securely as did the awkward drawing of a man's hands flourishing the cards. 'What does 'pneuamtic' mean when it comes to cards? I thought that was for tyres?'

'It was the very latest in modern technology then. Funny how the cutting edge dulls over time.'

'But what is a *pneumatic* card?' I licked the last of the Lagavulin from the tumbler and hoped more would magically appear.

Marinova narrowed her eyes at me. 'The card isn't pneumatic. The process by which they're printed is.' She ran a finger along the back of a card where four ladies in pink sat looking very Greek at one another. I suppose they were meant to be seductive, but they just seemed to be showing off their smooth underarms. 'See? Herringbone finish. As it says on the tin, 'Easy shuffling, perfect dealing.''

'So that's why you use them?'

'No, because they were my nana's I use them.' She held the pack up to her cheek a moment. 'Hello, nana.'

I feared for a moment that the cards might answer back and heard the thinnest echo of a response but I don't think it was actually audible to anyone but me. 'So carrying on a tradition.'

'Just like you.'

I snorted a little at that. 'Auntie Vera wasn't exactly the most noble of practitioners.'

'It's a trade inclined to lead one to fakery. Too much truth slices you to ribbons.' With lazy movements she began to shuffle the deck, her hands most gentle. The movements mesmerised me.

'I don't know. I think I just come from a long line of flash swindlers.'

Marinova offered a rare grin. 'It doesn't do to offer the truth too nakedly. People will take advantage. Hide it in a story, dress it up with baubles, but never hand it over for nothing. No one will thank you for it anyway.'

I sighed. 'Can I have more whisky to soften the blow?'

'No.' She began to put the cards down on the bar in an arrangement unfamiliar to me. I followed the revelation of each card with a meaningless hum until she shushed me. I can tell you I didn't like seeing the Queen *and* ace of spades show up. But I didn't understand her layout at all.

'Are you just making it up as you go along?' I finally asked, taking in the snaky pattern that met her satisfaction.

'I simply trust the cards.' She took a moment to gaze upon the bouquet before her.

'I'm fucked, aren't I?'

'Is it yourself you're asking for?'

I felt a pang. 'I suppose not.' The cards looked even more ominous now. 'I'm not liking the looks of that ace.'

'It's not a good thing, I'd say.'

'Is this her?' I pointed to the queen. 'I'm not liking the looks of it but at least she's away from the ace.'

'You're so accustomed to your little deck.'

'Little?'

She shrugged. 'Which she are you meaning?'

I gaped at her then looked back at the cards. 'What?'

She tapped the queen of spades. 'That's your chav lady there.'

'Peaches?! Oh, then this ten of diamonds across her…?'

'Money. I suspect that what's crossing her is her former husband's efforts.'

'Not too surprising that. But I haven't seen her lately and I was wondering—'

'It's not a good sign. Your worst fears realised.' Her voice remained stubbornly toneless. 'Look at that four of clubs.'

I didn't like the sound of that at all. A sinking feeling began to drag at my innards. 'But—I don't see how—'

'You'd know better than I.' Marinova pointed to the card obscured by the black ace. 'I'm a bit more concerned about this one.'

'Two of hearts? What could that—' I stopped as my throat closed up on me. 'No.'

'You asked.'

'But I didn't... I never said...' I shut my mouth and stared sullenly. 'Two of hearts.'

'I don't choose the cards, you do.' Marinova's eyes shined with something I didn't want to name.

'Helen. She's in danger, serious danger and I don't know how to help.'

'You do though. You already have the answers.' She tapped another card: nine of hearts. 'If you are willing to admit to the truth, there are ways to surmount these obstacles.'

I stared in silence. I was still trying to wrap my head around the two of hearts. 'Are you sure...?'

'Are you?'

'Is there a card that represents me?'

My dark haired beauty gave me a strange look and then turned over another card from the deck.

The joker. Of course. His squat figure grimaced at me, reminding me of Mr Punch for some reason, or maybe that was just the feeling in my gut. 'Beautiful.'

'And this one for your action.' Marinova turned another card across it. 'Unless you plan to remain the Fool.'

I stared at the last card. I couldn't decide if I liked it or not. 'You've been helpful.'

'I know.' She poured me another measure of Lagavulin and I drank it far too quickly to fully enjoy the peaty goodness. My hands shook a little. I didn't like that feeling, but I liked even less the insistent pulse of warning that knocked against my skull and urged me on.

To what?

'Don't try to jump over your own shadow,' Marinova said, her voice as gentle as forgiveness.

'You are blessed among our people.' I said, almost absently, for something like an idea had begun to scratch at the edges of my brain pan.

'You have made my head crazy.'

'You have broke my heart.' I gave her a wan smile, tipped my imaginary hat and turned on my heel. I muttered 'slainté' to the Irishman drinking alone, who crossed himself reflexively. Must have been something in my eye.

I took slow steps toward home and for once did not dip my hand to my pocket to check my reserves or lack thereof but kept my eyes on my feet and my thoughts from churning only with the most resolute concentration. Surely such unusual efforts must have showed on my face. Jinx opened the door with a look of surprise.

'Any messages?' He shook his head, yet that didn't seem to be the end of the conversation. Jinxy gave a nervous look over his shoulder.

'What?'

His eyes widened at me. I knew the look. Something had spooked him. When I say something had spooked this hulk of a man who had worked with me and spook central for far too long a time, it was bound to be something beyond your usual spookiness.

Terrific.

'Where?'

He pointed to the room in question. I sighed. 'Tell me the moment she gets here. Or calls, I suppose she might call.' Jinx nodded and then grabbed my arm impulsively. 'Now, now,' I reassured him and maybe myself. 'All will be well and all will be well and all manner of thing shall be well.' Crazy old Julian, as if she knew what she were talking about. She wished for her own death as a birthday present. I had other plans myself. I wouldn't stop my carriage for him and I wouldn't be looking for a lift anytime soon if I could help it.

I looked at the door to the parlour with some trepidation. The dull roar of what waited within already whispered that I ought to hit the dust and forget all about this, in fact why not book a holiday to Cornwall as soon as possible and disappear?

Instead I found my backbone, twisted the knob and strode in like a man in charge.

That lasted for all of a minute I think. The cacophony drilled my brain like a military tattoo. I put my hands to my ears, but the sounds not being audible it helped not a jot. 'SHUT UP!'

In vain my shouts. I tried to think, *What would Auntie Vera do?* Astonishingly, I had a thought. 'PLEASE JOIN THE QUEUE!' I grabbed at a wispy figure and parked her in front of me. 'What's the damage, dear?' My hope was that the others might fall into place behind her. I squinted, doing my best to make out her face, but I hoped what I saw wasn't like her living visage. Poor thing.

'Down down down, my mind... blank...' she muttered.

'Eh?' Even as I rolled my eyes, something itched at my mind.

'...spinning round and round...' Her head seemed to want to follow suit, lolling on her insubstantial neck.

'Look if you're just going to sing old pop songs at me—' and that's when I remembered. The old drunk in my cell; that was the song he was singing, too. Wanda bloody Jackson. Was it back on the charts? Pushing it for Christmas number one with a *really* early start?

I closed my eyes and listened, truly listened to the room. And then I started singing it and we were all in harmony, deep in that funnel of love. I could feel the chaotic crackle of energy reduce at once. I hadn't realised just how keyed up I had become, too, until my shoulders released and dropped down back to where they belonged. I opened my eyes again. The shimmering figures swum before me, calmer but still confusing to me.

I tried to use my most soothing voice and reached out to the young woman before me. 'What's this all about then?'

'Funnel...' she repeated, her wan face stretching with the word. 'Down down down...'

'Let's not get another sing song going,' I warned. I looked beyond this spook to the next one, an amorphous and some-what stodgy figure behind her. Impossible to guess gender, but it seemed more substantial. 'You, what can you tell me about this business?'

The figure eased through the mists of her predecessor and faced me. 'Hear the screams. The funnel grows. If we tarry…'

I closed my eyes again. This was not helping any. 'Look, have any of you seen Peaches?'

A murmur of sound began, slowly swelling and with it, a sense of dread. Hands on me, on my arms, on my head and the weightless press of them annoyed and unsettled me in equal degree.

'Look, if you don't know anything—' The muttering began in earnest then. Between the murmurs and the hands I began to feel as if a powerful wave were washing over me and I gasped for breath, a sense of panic barely contained.

To hell with that: a sense of panic filled my veins like the finest dust, goosing my pulse and making my heart go at it hammer and tongs. I had to fight the urge to up sticks and flee. You can't begin to imagine how those uncanny voices shiver up your spine. My hands were shaking like the worst of withdrawals. I'm not sure what kept me in my chair other than that strange bit of fondness I had developed for the irascible Peaches. 'Has she passed onto the, er, next… place?'

More cries of the funnel and down down down and then it hit me with the force of a careering lorry. Down down down in the funnel of the white rabbit, weren't it? 'Is that it? Is she taken? Did they get her?' They all wailed together like mad banshees, a sound I recognised as both grief and horror, because the same cry got squeezed out of my throat too. I felt as if my bonce would explode with the force of it, it was too much and then I did break away, I ran out into the hall, slamming the door behind me.

And ran into Saunders.

'For fuck's sake!'

'What?' She shoved me away from her and we both regarded one another balefully with alarm and uncertainty.

Then in unison: 'Where have you been?'

'What the hell's going on?' I rubbed my face briskly trying to recover my composure to some extent because I could see the shocked look on her face. I suspected the same expression was on my own face. 'Fuck me.'

'Not without a change of wardrobe,' Saunders said quietly, a tentative smile making a brief appearance on her lips.

I stared at her dumbfounded, then all at once I saw my own ignorance, stupidity and hopelessness and I started to laugh and laugh and laugh. Before long I was also coughing and choking and doubled over trying to catch my breath while Saunders pounded me on my back. I finally collapsed on the floor and, to my great surprise, began to sob.

I suppose more than anything I might have said that upset Saunders. 'What is it? Tell me!'

'They got Peaches,' I said, the words torn from my throat with ragged force. Somehow saying it out loud made it ever worse, as always. Tears stung my eyes.

Saunders' brow wrinkled. 'The spooks?'

'They're not spooks and no, not them.'

'Who then? Not...? But how?'

'Help me up.' I felt so shaky, as if my legs might not hold me up. Saunders grabbed my offered arm and half-dragged me to my feet once more. I swayed but stayed up. 'I-I think it was my fault, for going there, going near to... that place. That's what all these wraiths are trembling at, fearing they'll be next.'

'Did they just... erm, hoover her up?' Saunders seemed to hover on the edge of doubt. I suppose I should be grateful that she had at least accepted the reality of Peaches if not her fate.

Silly as the concept sounded, that pretty much nailed it as far as I could tell. 'I think that's how it kind of works.' Her look changed from doubt to surprise. 'That's what they were telling me in there,' I said, hooking my thumb over my shoulder back at the reading room. 'They were singing that same song, you know the one?'

'Which one? I just got here and I heard no singing.'

'Sarcasm, I remember that now. Wanda Jackson, 'Funnel of Love'. The Fall even covered it some time ago.'

'Funnel of Love?'

'Yeah.'

Saunders made a sound of annoyance. 'You're going to have to explain it better than just mentioning a pop song.'

'More a sort of rockabilly, really.' A severe look from Saunders and I realised what she meant. 'It's like a funnel that drags them into it.'

'The factory.'

'Warhol?' I think my head was ready to roll off my shoulders.

'No, no, the warren. That's what they call the place down on the docks officially: I just think of it as the factory now because of you. I have an appointment to go there.'

My head was pounding. 'We need some tea.' I turned and ambled down the corridor until I found Jinx reading *The Beano* and roused him to make a cuppa. Saunders trailed me into the kitchen. I sat down and put my head into my hands. After a moment I felt her hand on my shoulder. I can take anything but kindness. That gentle touch just about broke me. My eyes were still red, for fuck's sake. I wasn't going to blubber again. I needed something more in my veins. But I couldn't bring myself to move.

All the buried things filled the room with silence until Jinxy set the mugs before us, an unusually intense look on his face. I hadn't seen such an expression on his easy-going puss since the old battle days. Everything was out of sorts. Bad mojo.

But there are all kinds of magic. Ah, tea. It may not solve all life's problems but it does tend to make them a little more bearable.

'So, the factory,' Saunders started off.

'That day we were there…'

'They sucked away Peaches?' It clearly pained her to say it but having said it out loud, I suspected she found it a little easier to believe.

'I think so. I haven't heard her since and they all say the same thing, sing it really.' I took another gulp of tea. 'I feel responsible, it's all my fault.'

'She chose to haunt you,' Saunders suggested.

'She was gunned down in front of me. I'm not sure that counts as much of a choice. Bad enough fate that, let alone being sucked up into some kind of fear engine.' Poor Peaches, even in the afterlife things were dire. 'I probably seemed like the safest harbour—or at least the biggest beacon. I miss her and I have to figure out how to help her out. And all the others, too. What they're doing is more awful than anything in this life.' I shuddered again involuntarily.

'Well, I don't know, but I trust that you're right about it being what it is. So I did what I could to arrange my being there as soon as possible.'

'Is that a good thing?'

She shrugged. 'I realised they weren't going to let me in too quickly. Insiders have to be well vetted. But I did have one card to play: my sister's ghost.' Saunders looked fierce as if daring me to challenge her. I had no intention of doing so.

'Bait,' was all I said.

'Yeah and they took it. They were keen once I mentioned being haunted. I felt like a cartoon of a hot meal.'

Jinxy fired up the kettle again for refills. I tried to kick-start my thinking again. 'So how do they describe it? As helping you? Or the ghost?'

Saunders laughed, a dry snort. 'Actualising, advancing, clearing the aura—no, that's not right. They use a different term. 'Environment' I think it was. Their rhetoric is self-consciously scientific. Cleansing, draining—various words for removing the chaff.'

'They know you have something they want.'

'Wanna come with me?'

'I thought you'd never ask.' I rubbed my eyes. 'We need a plan.'

'I don't suppose we can just jump out and say 'Get 'em!' can we?'

Things must be real bad if Saunders was trying to be funny, though I appreciated her knowing *Ghostbusters*. Somehow I had pigeonholed her as rather more highbrow. 'I need some kind of shield if I'm going back into that place.' I shivered at the thought of that murderous hole. I could still feel the shrieks in my bones.

'Shield?'

'Dust and plenty of it. Plus some kind of downer to ground me.'

Saunders digested this information while Jinxy refilled the mugs. His expression had the same flavour of disapproval that Saunders' did. 'Is that wise?'

'I'm not sure I can withstand the onslaught otherwise. You have no idea how horrible it is.' I did shiver then. A sweat broke out on my forehead. 'And I need to restock soonish. Dust ain't cheap either.' I added glumly.

'Where do you get it?' Saunders reluctance suggested she wasn't sure she wanted the answer at all.

'Oh, the usual source,' I said trying not to sound too cagey. The 'usual source' was a feral sort of gentleman who could be found in the darker recesses of Crystal Palace Park near those ridiculous prehistoric dinosaur thingees and who looked more than a bit dodgy, something like a wood sprite drawn by Rackham with a nervous, intoxicated mien that surely had nothing to do with sampling his own wares.

Not that I had any room to speak.

Don't judge me, as they say on mid-morning television. The thought of braving that atrocity factory again filled me with the shivers. It would be easier altogether just to surrender to the dust. But poor Peaches! And damn that Marinova—the cards.

Jack of spades, she told me, he was pointing the way forward, crossing the Fool, er, Joker with purpose. Huh, someone made a big error. A Dylan song danced on the edge of my memory, tantalising but not quite present. Surely this could not end well. I finally noticed that Saunders still gaped at me, clearly expecting some kind of response.

'What?' Man of few words, me. Most of them unintelligible.

'So... what's our plan?'

'Oh, right. Plan.' Could she tell I was stalling? Yes, surely. 'Right then, first I replenish, then we head off—'

'We? Just the two of us?'

'We meaning Jinx and me, because maybe Jinx would offer us some insurance, though he is rather a giveaway. I might call Coburn just to leave word, you know.' Were we really going to do this? Charge in like John Wayne or Gary Cooper on white horses? Did they ride white horses? No, that was the Lone Ranger fella. White horses, white rabbit—I don't think I was ready to think about that. A bus ride would give me time to think. I couldn't think with Saunders giving me those cow eyes.

'So... I wait here until you get back?' Saunders didn't seem too pleased with that notion, judging by the moue her lips made. Very nice lips. Damn her anyway.

'You could do more research. There must be some research on this kind of thing, somewhere? Even in crackpot sorts of places they must get some notion of how they're doing what they're doing which is a kind of crackpot thing after all.' Surely that sounded more sensible in her ears than in mine. Anyway she nodded, though looking more than a tad bit sceptical.

'You'll phone me?' Saunders cocked an eyebrow at me with her usual skill. 'You wouldn't go in alone?'

I shuddered. 'No, never. I'd not go in at all if I could avoid it.' A sick feeling settled in the pit of my stomach. *I'll think about that later, after the dust.* I patted my pockets to make sure I had my Oyster card, then realised I would need some cash. The uncanny folk might be otherworldly but they appreciated foldin' money as much as any mortal when it came to living in this realm and yer man had strange sartorial tastes that would put Vince Noir on his mettle. It was often their way when they chose to inhabit this world.

Why they would choose to do so, I am uncertain. If they'd give me the map, I would run through the bluebells and never look back.

'Right, I'm off to catch my bus,' I said, uncertain whether I should try to kiss Saunders on the cheek or something, as an excuse for a farewell.

She looked at me and then away as if the awkwardness were catching. 'Tatty bye.'

I stumbled out the door, closing it behind me with a muttered curse aimed at the vagaries of fate perhaps, and immediately tripped over the ginger cat, who looked at me where I fell as if I had somehow deeply offended her. 'Did I inconvenience you?' I grumbled as I waited for the wind to return to my surprised lungs. I had just about struggled back to my feet once more when a couple of pairs of Docs approached and when I looked up I saw they were attached to some of Dockmuir's heavies and I sighed.

'Collecting for the blind?' I barely had time to get the requisite quip out before one of them punched me in the gut and they bustled me into the white van again and I sank down to the floor with what very nearly approximated a sense of relief.

At least I didn't have to make any decisions for a while.

The pain in my gut had begun to subside when we arrived at headquarters. At least I assumed it must be headquarters because it was some kind of multi-storey car park that was completely dark and the two bruisers hustled me along to a stairwell that was equally dimly lit and then down a corridor that screamed 'servants only' and then through a door into an enormous office that shouted 'executive' with a belligerent tone from its blandly fashionable minimalism to its panoramic view of the Old Smoke.

It's good to be the king.

They threw me to my knees and I wondered at the usefulness of prayer while I was down there but before I had a chance to ponder the likelihood of a greater good or greater evil when we seemed to be doing so well without, Dockmuir walked in from the outer office with a swagger of the ten pence variety and a smile that suggested I had a lot of suffering ahead.

'Mr Draygo,' the mogul said as he seated himself in his overstuffed leather chair. No Conran this, surely. 'You are trouble, I'm afraid.'

'I don't mean to be. I just want to live a quiet life, collecting stamps and living off the fat of the land.' I did try to sound as humble as possible. No pride for me. As if it would make any difference with this mad old man with his scrawny neck, his shiny pate and his expensive clothes and his cheap cheap shoes.

'What's this I hear, you looking into places where you ought not go, seeing people you ought have nothing to do with. Or did we not have a chat about this just the other day?' So smug, so condescending: if I didn't hate him already I certainly would come to do so in a matter of minutes.

'I don't know what you mean,' I said truthfully enough. Let him tell me how much he knew as it might be less than I thought. I knew I was taking my chances, but there you are. Throw the bones: *I am the dice man, the hauls of the crime man*...surely that wasn't right, but somehow panic impeded my recollection of obscure lyrics.

Dockmuir sighed and one of his heavies took that as a sign to kick me in the gut. As I doubled over making the sound known as *oof*, I made a mental note to compliment the good doctor on his footwear. Took a beating and kept on repeating—or was that gave a beating? Hard to think properly while your guts screamed in agony.

'We know you went to see that whore,' Dockmuir continued, his tone suggesting a weary patience. 'I've got eyes and ears everywhere.'

Ah, Burnsie. No doubt that lowlife turncoat had passed along news of our visit to Raphaelita's flat. Not good, yet not at all surprising either. And if there was good news it was that such might be the extent of his knowledge. If he didn't yet know we'd been sniffing around the warren, so much the better. 'That damn Burnsie,' I muttered.

'A man with a conscience,' Dockmuir tutted. 'You should learn from his example.'

If I were a hero in a classic old British film, I would doubtless declare my refusal with quiet intensity and a trembling lip then make some speech about the little people and their fine example as they fought in their little ways against the creeping rot of fascism. 'I shall endeavour to do so,' I hastily promised in hopes of staving off another kick to the innards.

'What did you hope to find in there?' Illusions of kindness departed; his voice flashed its steel core.

'I hoped to find my friend Raphaelita. For some reason rumour had it that she was in a bit of a scrape and could use a hand. We just stopped by to see if she were all right.'

There was no immediate addition of pain as Dockmuir seemed to consider this response. 'And has she been in contact in any way since then?'

I did my best to conceal my sense of relief. 'Not a sausage.' *Maybe she's still alive!* I certainly hoped the wily film fan had escaped this old bugger or she'd wind up just as dead as Babyface had—and looking no prettier. 'I left word with some friends around her usual haunts but not a peep has been heard from her. What did she do to you?'

That earned me a half-hearted cuff on the head; hardly worth the bother for the stars it created. At this point the dull throb of aches throughout my body sang a dirge of despair. One more blow might just crumble what was left of the connective tissue, I feared.

Dockmuir must have been considering my words. 'I suspect she's off on a holiday so you ought not bother her. Neither you nor your nosey parker friend. Do I make myself clear?'

'As the proverbial crystal,' I hastened to assure him. 'My friend has a new obsession requiring long hours of research in St Pancras, obscure old texts, nothing in the modern era, very busy, very. We're all busy, miles to go before we kip and all that hip hip, pip.'

'The cheaper the psychic, the gaudier the patter,' Dockmuir said with a sniff. I had to give him a little extra credit for that. But he wasn't done. There was some kind of doubt, bordering very nearly on nerves, reflected in his eyes. 'Good to know she's found a hobby. So, nothing to do with the white rabbit?'

How well can I hide surprise? On a scale from one to ten,

where would you place your efforts at concealment? I might rate a seven on a good day, I'd like to pride myself on that.

This, of course, was not a good day. 'White rabbit? 'I'm late, I'm late' sort of white rabbit?' I wrinkled my brow in what was doubtless a grotesque parody of confusion. Gaudier the patter indeed.

Dockmuir got up from his chair and sauntered over to me. He had a half-smile on his lips as he did so, which made me a little wary. I wasn't entirely surprised when he grabbed my obviously-in-need-of-a-trim hair to wrench my face up toward his. 'You wouldn't be lying to me now, would you, Draygo?'

'Rabbit out of a hat?' I tried, trying not to look either too disconcerted, nor too intimidated while wincing against the pain not from the hair itself being pulled but the increased roar from the various aches reawakened by a newly awkward posture. 'I don't know. Harvey?'

Dockmuir frowned. 'Harvey who?'

'Harvey, the púca.' I closed my eyes as my vision had begun to swim.

'You've lost me, mate.' At least he let go of my hair then and I collapsed with a grateful exhalation even though the heap I landed in was a heap of pain.

'Classic film with Jimmy Stewart: a drunk, hangs around with a giant invisible white rabbit no one else can see.' I could hear myself babbling.

'Oh, I know that one,' the Mancunian heavy offered. 'My nan's fave film.'

Dockmuir chuckled. It had the ring of genuine amusement. 'Sounds like the story of your life, Draygo.'

'Indeed,' I muttered, too exhausted by the pain to do more than send a brief, heartfelt prayer of thanks to Elwood P. Dowd and his coney pal.

'Dump him somewhere convenient,' Dockmuir told his Doc squad. 'I see you again, you won't be too happy. And neither will I.'

With that I was seized once more and dragged from the room without ceremony, bounced back down the stairs to the van. I was grateful that I passed out for a time—how long a time, I couldn't have told you—and awakened once more only when they prepared to dump me without so much as a farewell kiss.

Where was I this time? Hard to say at first as I blinked in the sudden dazzle of sunlight. The renewed stab of various pains told me the surface I'd landed on was hard, but the murmur of traffic and people told me at least it wasn't in the middle of nowhere. I let the air return to my lungs and then blinked around me.

I stumbled to my feet. Nothing looked familiar—it could be any of a hundred streets somewhere in this dirty old town. I shambled down the pavement frightening small children (well, one) until I came to the next corner and took a gander around. Nothing jogged my memory but I saw the welcome sign that meant escape. Apparently I was at West India Quay on the DLR, a place I had never actually managed ever to be in this city. At least I knew it was East. With luck I even had enough left on the Oyster to get me back home.

As I swayed along with the crowd heading into the station thoughts began to return to my overtaxed noggin. The need for dust took first place naturally. I patted my pockets and found a couple more painkillers that were not going to be enough, but the notions taking shape didn't stop there. I was getting angry. It took a while, eh? I didn't have a lot in this world, and I couldn't say I cared much—and it was more than likely that this plane would be better off without me.

I would die unmourned, unloved, obscurity my middle name, no plaques, no wake, no tears shed.

Because I had fucked up badly—no, everyone fucks up badly. What I hadn't done was make it right. We all have chances to do that as well. I felt the boy who could be found ever at my elbow and looked down. It was a shock to see and know his face again. I had assiduously avoided his gaze for years now. Even in the roar of the tunnel I could hear the ticking of the one clock. It didn't always let you know when it needed rewinding. Sometimes it just stopped.

'I want to make it right,' I told him.

147

He looked up at me with the too dark eyes and said nothing. Maybe he couldn't speak. Maybe he was past speaking. Maybe he wanted to watch me suffer. I stared into his eyes. The sadness in his face stabbed my heart. I had forgotten how neat the black line of the fringe lay across his brow and the caterpillar arch of his two eyebrows. There was something in his expression beyond the sadness, something I couldn't quite put my finger on.

Impatience.

It was as if a key went into a lock but I couldn't quite turn it. *I'm late, I'm late.* The train came to a halt and it was my stop. I wandered off reluctantly, unwilling to meet his eyes again but feeling as if something had been returned to me. It couldn't be hope, but it might be something with a nice name like resolve.

I wanted to make a show of bursting through the door with dramatic effect but of course I didn't have my keys with me and anyway they must have thought I'd only gone for the dust. So I came up with a good opening question.

'Jinxy, what have we got as weapons?'

His surprise showed plainly on his plain face. It was accompanied by doubt.

'Weapons?' Saunders multiplied the doubt and added scepticism. 'I don't think we want weapons.'

'We do. I got hijacked by Dockmuir again. No, it's not that,' I added, taking in her doubting expression. 'I didn't get any dust, didn't get the chance. I'm going to have to go without for a little while longer. Yes, really.' I waved away her questions. If I didn't think about it no one else would, surely. 'He doesn't know we know, so I think we should act quickly before he does.'

'I don't know,' she said cautiously, exchanging a look with Jinx. 'Do we have a plan now?'

'We didn't before, so why have one now?' I laughed but it sounded a bit hollow even to my ears. 'We're going to have to feel our way along and figure out some way of getting to the heart of things, stopping that engine or whatsis, and letting them all go.'

'What if we can't?'

'We'll find a way!'

Saunders coughed. 'Look, an hour or so ago you were barely able to cope with the idea and now you've suddenly turned into Bruce Willis and suggesting weapons—'

'I'd prefer Jason Statham to play me in the movie version.'

'Hilarious. What the hell happened to you?'

I attempted to rein it in a bit. I could see she wasn't buying the sudden transformation. She wanted me to explain to her a little of what happened. What had happened? 'Apart from the whole routine beating by Dockmuir? Plenty, but not things I want to share. I know, Women's Hour argues I ought not to bottle things up or I'll explode, but I want to explode. I just want it to be a controlled explosion where it does some good. Like bring Dockmuir's warren crashing down. We can't allow this to continue. They've done a horrible thing and it's only going to get worse and put more people at danger. So we have to stop it.'

Saunders seemed to be measuring me. 'Can we do this?'

'We have to try.'

'What sort of weapons?'

'Now you're talking.' I rubbed my hands together, though truthfully I had absolutely no idea. 'Well, I have a gun. Jinxy has a gun—no, you do.' I corrected him as he shook his head slowly. 'It may be old but it works. But we need something else, too.' I turned on my heel and headed to the parlour. I wasn't keen to brave the noise and the grabbing hands that grab all they can, but there was something that might be useful.

I braced myself for the assault and charged on through the room ignoring the imprecations from all sides. I crossed to Auntie Vera's cabinet and undid the Chinese lock. I hadn't touched it in years and yet the complex system of sliding panels came back to me instantly. The cabinet was chockfull of bric-a-brac, a testament to Vera's packrat habit. Houdini might appreciate a gander through its contents as the better part of it contained all manner of séance tomfoolery, some of it handed down from Auntie Vera's aunties, some—rumour had it—going back to the time of Abelard and Heloise (not that said double-act had much to do with the spooky trade as far as I know).

I knew there were a couple of things that might come in handy, however. Finding them was a bit more of an issue. I closed my eyes and tried to picture the last time I'd been rifling through the shelves. I hadn't been more than about sixteen, of course too smart arse to be more than half-listening to Vera as she recounted the various tools and mementos. 'This one came from the Fox Sisters—not *those* Fox Sisters, but the ones who ran with the skulk in the midlands. Came over from Japan sometime in the sixteenth century. And this used to belong to John Dee.'

'But not that John Dee,' I had muttered with a smirk before she gave me a half-hearted backhand, spilling a little ash from her ever-present Woodbine.

'That John Dee, indeed, you little guttersnipe.' She sniffed. I only got called 'guttersnipe' when she was in a particularly good mood. Vera had made a killing at bingo the night before, something she didn't risk too often. People didn't believe in psychics (except when they did) but you didn't want to encourage too much thought about it.

'It's just a trick coin,' I said turning it over.

'Breathe on it.' She smirked at me. I looked up at her warily. I had seen enough to know not to trust her. More than once I had landed flat on my keister while she laughed like a banshee or should I say, a *ban-sidhe* as she was. 'Go on. It won't bite.' More sniggering.

I breathed on it and smoothed the surface with my thumb. The Latin inscription and Tiberius' head changed under my hands to a heaving nymph, legs splayed and back arched. I could almost hear her moan. Considering at that age a stray wind would have me up, I found it alluring. 'Can I keep this?'

She smacked the back of my head, which made me drop it. 'No, that's valuable. Earn some money first.' I didn't remember what we had been looking for that day. But I remembered that coin and how it felt suddenly warm under my fingers.

Old magic, you can't beat it. Not sure why I didn't go back and just swipe it.

But you didn't do that to Vera. Too likely to end in a kind of auntie-apocalypse. Maybe when we were through with all this business I'd find it again. Just for a keepsake.

It took a good bit of digging to sort out the useful from the kitsch. She had a lot of dreck saved 'just in case'—in case of what it was uncertain. Trinkets and tricks jumbled up with precious items of wealth beyond reckoning. Why had I never thought of looting this cabinet before? Auntie Vera's face arose before me just then. I knew precisely why.

'Ah ha!' At last, the spirit kettle. It looked like all the parts were intact as well. No oil in the burner, but that could be fixed easily. Regency craftwork on the copper gave it an elegant look despite the tarnish. The little stand for it looked well sturdy. And it looked normal enough—if a bit bulky. I was going to need some kind of carry bag. One of Vera's voluminous canvas ones ought to do, even if carpetbags had long gone out of fashion.

I poked around a bit longer, feeling something calling me, uncertain what I was looking for. Finally my hand located a smoky orb that crackled at my touch. I held it out toward the fading afternoon light to get a better look and tried to remember what Vera had said about it. There were a lot of items she used for set dressing that didn't really do much of anything. I could feel something inside it, but that could mean just about anything. I didn't know if it was a 'real' something or an ethereal one. I'd have to test it on Saunders.

She looked at it doubtfully when I handed it over to her. Jinxy looked curious, too, as he put another set of cups down at the kitchen table. 'What's this supposed to be?'

'It has an ancient name that I can't really pronounce,' I lied. Better than admitting I couldn't remember whether it had a name at all.

Saunders eyebrow suggested grave doubt anyway. 'What does it do?'

'Can you feel anything in it?'

'In it?' She inspected it closer up. 'Mexican jumping beans?'

'Very funny. Can you feel anything moving?'

That earned me a strange look. 'Moving? I can see light shifting a little. Is it some kind of crystal or whatnot? Quartz, that's it.'

'But you don't feel anything?' I could sense its movements increasing. The warmth of hands must be awakening it. Whatever it was. Judging by Saunders' reactions, something entirely ethereal.

'Sorry, no.' She handed it back. Jinxy nodded and I let him hold it for a wee while. His brow furrowed as he stared into its depths. He put his ear to it, then shrugged and gave it back. I wrapped it in a tea towel and put it in the bag with the spirit kettle and the gun. I had put the last bit of my dust in the bag too, after staring at it a little too long. I don't think I drooled, but maybe I was not entirely truthful.

'So what's the plan?' Saunders had Jinxy's gun. He had cleaned and oiled it carefully even though I could see he had real misgivings about employing it. Saunders seemed confident about carrying it. I wondered if that was bravado on her part.

'We go for your appointment, but late. I sneak in with you and find a place to hide and wait until they close. We let Jinxy in and then go down to the warren.'

'Okay, I see a few problems with this plan. What if they don't let me in? What if they don't let you in? What if Jinx is left waiting outside? What if they get word to Dockmuir?'

'What if the skies fall? We'll deal.'

She looked at me with a super large extra helping of scepticism. 'Speaking of dealing, what about you and your addiction and your withdrawal? I thought it was impossible to withstand the screams of that place? I remember what your face looked like.'

'I'm not saying it will be easy,' I gave a laugh that sounded hollow even to me. 'I think it may be easier in my right mind, so to speak, because I won't be as inclined to panic. And withdrawal makes me mean.'

'Look, I know you want to do something here, but I think we may be going off half-cocked here.'

'You have no idea what I want to do.' I could feel the boy at my elbow, silent yet insistent. 'What I have to do. It's an obscenity and it needs to be stopped. No one else can seem to see or hear it, which makes it my problem. Believe me, I don't want to have to do this. I really don't. But I can't not do it.' *Much as I've tried.*

'So what am I going to do?' Saunders looked annoyed and yet slightly eager, too.

'You're going to get us in.'

We took a cab to the docks. 'Might as well live it up, eh?' I joshed as we got in.

'Eat, drink and be merry for tomorrow—'

'Don't say it.' I felt a superstitious dread tingle along my spine. 'But I want to leave a message for Coburn before we go in. You know, just in case we need a rescue or... something.'

'Will he come?'

I exchanged a glance with Jinx who knew a lot more of the history between me and my former partner. Hell, he even knew the kid at my side—or had done. 'He will if he thinks there's trouble. We just don't want him coming too soon.'

'Before we get in?'

'Before we find something worth finding.' I was a bit worried about that; what if the factory couldn't be seen by anyone but me? It would be a bit of a hard sell. I watched the city slip past as we headed toward Tower Bridge. I never noticed how melancholy and small the Elephant and Castle looked when you were heading to an uncertain fate. I tried to remember what Marinova had said, remember the cards. I might be the Fool—er, Joker—but I had that Two of Hearts to keep track of.

Saunders kept her thoughts to herself. How I had come to enjoy that profile. Jinxy was drinking it in with a half-smile. I looked out the window again. It was too much to bear the light for long.

All too soon for my liking we were pulling up at the conference centre. 'Jinxy, you make yourself scarce for a time. We'll let you in after closing. Find the likely spots around back and be ready for the signal.'

The big lug nodded and walked off like he had nothing better to do than feed the pigeons. I had no worries about him, provided nobody waved something shiny in front of him. It should be alright, I told myself, everything should be just fine.

'Right then,' I muttered to Saunders as we walked up to the door, 'you try to get in and we'll play it by ear. I'll probably have to hide in a toilet somewhere and if you can slip away, do the same. If they close up around nine-ish we can plan to look around half past.'

'We should have checked their security forces. Do they have any beyond videos?' Saunders looked at me with a sudden scrutiny. 'Are you all right?'

The screams were horrible. Without the buffer of dust, I could hear them distinctly without the buzz of echo. I can say with confidence that I have never heard anything more disturbing, not even the scream of a small boy dying horribly though it was a close race. I needn't look down to know he was at my elbow, but even he seemed distracted by the wailing. 'Yeah, just dandy like candy.'

'Are you sure?' The concern in her face was palpable.

'No, but we must endeavour, eh?' If I stopped now I would never be able to keep on, so the feet must beat on the Mississippi mud. *Where did that come from?* Random phrases from the subconscious: not a good sign. I could feel the sweat on my palms. *Remember all the things Auntie Vera taught you. Block it all out.* At least for now.

For all our paranoia, the place inside seemed so normal as to squeak with boredom. The murmur of voices, the clatter of heels on the lino, and oh, the smiles from the people who didn't know what lay under their feet. I clocked two cameras trained on the entrance, but hoped for an after-the-fact-footage rather than a live feed. One could hope.

'Hi,' Saunders said in her best and brightest voice. 'I had

an appointment but I'm a bit late. A clearing I think they called it.'

'Your first time?' The receptionist gave a megawatt smile. 'Not clearing but a first aura inventory. We have to see what you have before we know what to eliminate. It feels so good to be cleansed of all that dross.'

She turned the smile on me and I gave her a weak return. 'I'm just here for moral support.'

'Yeah, he was—' Saunders didn't seem to know how to pass me off, bless her.

'Oh, that's all right.' Ms Cheerio said with a sparkle. 'You can both go in. A lot of people are nervous the first time. There's nothing at all to be worried about, but new things. We want everyone to be comfortable.'

Well, that was a stroke of luck. Probably. The effort of keeping the deaf ear was making me sweat. I could feel a trickle down my spine and was glad I had my moth-eaten old Savile Row topper over my shirt. We sat down in the waiting area until the 'technician' was free—apparently finishing up with another unfortunate. Saunders picked up a magazine to flip through it, trying to look at ease. I did my best not to perspire at an ever-increasing rate and not to let the panic take hold of me.

This must be what it's like to be waiting for your turn at bat, when the bat will be turned on you and the screams of the bloke before you let you know what's in store. They say the most important part of desire is anticipation; it's the same for torture. Hearing might even be worse than seeing what's happening. What you see, you can dissemble; what you hear, you can only imagine.

Imagination is ruthless.

A hand on my knee: Saunders' hand. I look up at her and the kindness in her eyes is almost too painful to bear. 'It's bad, isn't it?'

I did my best to smile. It was probably a feeble attempt. 'I don't want to talk about it, not really. I don't think I can. Not coherently anyway.' Ground ground ground, as Auntie Vera would say. Put down your roots into the earth and don't let 'em drag you away. It suddenly struck me that the ongoing wails either meant a continuous supply—which even at the rate of modern death, seemed unlikely—or else a continuous torture.

Which meant suffering without end—not good, of course, but with possibilities. I looked at the kid who followed me everywhere. He was scared. His long face and big eyes reflected the panic I felt inside that I was trying to keep tamped down. If I had lost Peaches here, why not him?

I think the answer lay in his tenacious grip on my elbow. I'd not paid him any attention for years now until all the business with Peaches made me open up my head again. But he had clung there persistently, I always thought, to punish me. I had relived his death a hundred times or more, and hated myself every time. A moment's inattention and it was done.

And I was undone. Jawbone of an ass indeed. I never could shut up when I needed to—and before you ask, no I wasn't on the dust or anything else back then. It was just my own self-manufactured drug of what's next, what's happening, always needing the juice of excitement, but never here, never in the moment, not even behind the wheel.

Rameth was all of ten, a skinny kid. His big brown eyes shone with fear now, not that panic of that night, surprise even and that tiny body flung so far in the dark on that quiet street to lie even more quietly as we sobbed and waited on the wail of the siren but it was too late too late too late. And finding in my favour as an accident didn't help and the snickering nicknames didn't help and the big eyes at my elbow every time I turned didn't help and the only thing that did was the dust.

'We're ready for you now,' the receptionist said brightly and I rubbed my eyes like I was tired, and I was. Saunders looked at me strangely and I got up, but I took a deep breath and I looked at him squarely. His gaze was hungry but it was not starved for revenge or retribution. He was so alone. Think of it, you idiot, ten years old and thrust into the luminiferous ether on his own, nobody around but you. And you ignored him all that time.

So I took his hand.

I didn't care how it might look. I walked behind Saunders who followed at the shoulder of the receptionist, keeping up a chatter of friendly meaningless conversation as you do. I was scared for the little fella, I was scared for us. Yet for the first time in years, I didn't feel like there was a silver knife piercing my heart.

Just a vice crushing my head. The sound grew louder as we walked along the corridor. I was afraid what we might see inside, but as she showed us through the door there was a pair of nice young clean-cut people at a table with a surprisingly pretty looking terrible machine on it.

'Hi, I'm Rosie and this is Fred.' They shook hands with Saunders as we sat down. With one hand holding the boy and the other my carpet bag, I didn't have a hand to spare. The two of them didn't seem to take it amiss. They were two of the most blandly pale people I had ever seen in the city. They matched their surroundings. Apart from the singular machine, the room had just the four chairs, standard practice corporate soothing green walls and some framed Turner prints, which seemed a bit artsy for the organisation, but maybe they wanted the comfort of the familiar. Who in London didn't know Turner's light? There was only one bit of propaganda, a simple block letter epigram on the wall behind the machine: CHOOSE RATIONAL LOVE. I didn't know what to make of that.

'I'm just here for moral support,' I said feeling uncertain. How could they bear the cacophony? Did they not hear it? Surely they could at least sense it? I held tight to little Rameth's hand as he stood between me and Saunders. The pull on him was strong and he was terrified, but I wouldn't let go. I owed him that much.

'It's a simple process,' Rosie said, clearly the senior partner in the patter. 'We clear the energetic aura around your head. A lot of it is just psychic noise you've gathered over the years.'

'With this thing?' Saunders pointed to the machine. It was

a strange Rube Goldberg-esque mixture of old and new. The console in front of Saunders looked like some kind of video game thingee with handholds and screens that had dials with numbers. The body of the machine it connected to through green wires, however, looked a lot older and I wondered if Dockmuir had an Auntie Vera, too—one with a greater skill for tinkering instead of magpie fingers.

'What is this exactly?' I asked trying to sound curious rather than accusatory. 'I mean, how does it work?'

Rosie's smile came down a few notches but shined anyway. 'The Aetheric Clarifier. It's an energy circulator at heart. Moving the troublesome excess energy clouding your consciousness so you can think rationally and freely.'

'And where does it go?'

'In here.' Fred pointed to the big round-bottomed flask in the belly of the beast. It seemed to be the extent of his knowledge, though he smiled seraphically as was apparently his wont.

'But after that?'

Rosie handed him a brochure. On the cover it said *How to be Free*. I could see the appeal in that. 'You'll find most of the answers in here. If you watch while your friend undergoes the session, I think you'll be guided to discover more. You'll find what we've all discovered: It's good to have a clean slate.'

Wow, she could sling the old rhetoric. 'It's not… dangerous?'

Rosie laughed and yet the sound felt somehow practiced, too. 'Oh heavens, no! It's completely harmless, beneficial even—in fact we have shown through extensive experimentation that the process has even wider reaching healthy effects than we initially imagined.'

'Harmless?'

Her smile was getting a bit chilly around the edges. 'Completely.'

'Even to the ghosts?' I had to ask, if only to see how much she knew. Or least how much she would tell.

Her smile offered pity now. 'There are no 'ghosts' as you call them. Old superstition that wanted to believe that people lived on after death; it caused us to put faces on interfering aetheric energies, like a child imagining a malignant spirit hiding under the bed.'

'I see.' I held Rameth's hand ever tighter.

'You need to embrace rational love,' Rosie said, more gently now. 'See the world with clear eyes. The cloud of superstition befogs our daily lives until then.'

'So that's what the white rabbit teaches,' I said, as much to Saunders as to the stooges.

'Just relax,' Saunders said, worried I was upsetting the apple cart and our whole plan, which come to think of it I might be. But I noticed that Rameth had also grabbed her hand and was clinging to it tightly. I'm not sure she noticed. It's a natural enough thing to take a child's hand. He was a smart kid.

'I'm just trying to understand what this is all about. If you don't think the energy you remove is important, why do you collect it? Why not just destroy it?'

Rosie looked at me with the indulgence saved for idiot children and stupid old men. 'We have to dissipate it safely. You can't just release that destructive energy any old where. Otherwise you'll just return it to the same damaging places. It clings to people, you know, like static electricity. You really need to read that pamphlet. It will help clarify a lot of the things you need to know. If you choose to be free, that is. There's a lot to learn from our system.'

'I know what we learned from Alice.' I said, reaching into the canvas bag at my feet.

Rosie frowned. 'What did we learn from Alice?'

'Stay in the dream. Kill the white rabbit.' I lifted up the gun and leveled it at Rosie. Her eyes bulged. She raised her hands like it was a stick up.

After a tick, Fred followed suit. That was more like it.

Saunders tried to keep her expression neutral, 'Where does the energy go when you've sucked it out of the people?'

'I—I don't know.'

I sighed. 'Let me try again. What do you do with that flask there when you've finished a session?'

She nodded nervously toward the door behind them. 'We take it to the Concatenator.'

More jargon: this Dockmuir had the whole business ironed out. You needed a playbook to keep up with the acolytes. Oh, wait—that's exactly what they had. 'Righteo. Let's go.'

'Go?' She gaped at me.

'To the Concatenator.' I felt absurd saying the words and wondered if I had turned into some kind of caped crusader. 'Let's all go.' I waved the gun in a way that I hoped would be taken as menacing. Truth to tell I was getting a mite short-tempered. Rosie gave me a baleful look, but pulled a key ring from her pocket and walked over to open the door. Fred followed her and I nodded to Saunders, who let go of Rameth's hand and ambled after them down the corridor, flexing her fingers. I closed the door behind us as the fluorescent tubes flickered.

Saunders turned to whisper to me. 'Whose hand was I holding?'

'I'll explain later,' I said, hoping I wouldn't have to do that. At the other end of the hall, Rosie unlocked another door. That was an awful lot of security for energy that 'didn't matter' or I was much mistaken. I stepped forward to bring the gun nearer to Rosie. 'Move nice and slow; no tricks now.'

As if I didn't already feel like a walking, talking cliché, that certainly clinched it.

I herded them through the door into the white room. It didn't look quite so sterile as the interrogation room, less for show and more for business, not to mention a bit messier. There were a couple of empty round-bottom flasks like the one in the belly of the other machine in a rack by a small stainless steel sink, a table with a few chairs around it and in pride of place, The Concatenator.

How to describe it? It was a mix of shiny and mechanical, tech and magic. There was some kind of metal wheel and a pulley connected to wire-wrapped magnets I think—they certainly pulled at my old gun—with wires dipping into some kind of oversised beaker of fluid. It all seemed to be sealed inside a vacuum. I remembered going to an exhibit back in school days at the Science Museum that featured dynamos and early magnetic engines. This was the engine that ran the warren: the funnel. Down, down, down, it dragged them.

The most obvious aspect of it for me was one the rest of them seemed oblivious to: the muttering hum of voices that it gathered and twisted. Rameth trembled. He and I were the only ones who appeared to feel what was happening—the way that people's most intimate memories, emotions, lives and dreams were being wrung out, twisted together and rolled into a kind of energetic ball with all the pain that sort of violence could create. I thought of just switching it off, but wondered what worse would happen then—besides its noise was only part of the problem.

That was no comparison to what I could hear from next door: horrible screaming. What were they doing to the gathered power? I didn't know, but it couldn't be good. Rameth struggled against it, writhing in my grip, not desiring to be loose, but so harrowed by the sound that he could not keep still. Tremors wracked my limbs, which I did my best to control without much success.

The other three were staring at me. It probably didn't seem to them like all that much time had passed, though it seemed ages to me. The strain might not yet be showing, but I certainly felt it.

'What's in the next room?' I finally managed to say, pointing to where the wires from the machine escaped.

Rosie shrugged, looking sullen. 'I don't know. I don't have a key to that.'

'Right.' I turned to Saunders. 'We need to bind and gag them.'

'With what?' She gestured helplessly.

'I dunno. Can you find something?' I held the gun on the two rabbitters while Saunders poked around under the sink and in the cupboards above it. 'You two. Sit.' I indicated the chairs. It would make it easier to tie them assuming something could be found. Saunders managed to turn up a couple of ragged tea towels and a coil of rubber-coated copper wire that matched the stuff used in the machine. Lacking any kind of wire cutter, she just looped it around each of them and their chair, one after the other.

'Oh, you're not going to stick that nasty thing in my mouth,' Rosie said with obvious consternation.

'Yes,' Saunders said simply. 'Yes, I am.'

Their eyes followed us around the room, Rosie's bulging with ire, Fred's mostly with disbelief and confusion. 'So now what?'

I shrugged. 'I want to see what's going on in the next room. That's where all the screaming is coming from.'

'Screaming?' Her brow furrowed with dismay. 'I-I can't hear it.'

'I know.'

Saunders looked down at my hand clutching Rameth's tightly, but said nothing. 'Should we try to get Jinx in here?'

'It would be helpful, but I suspect we don't have time if these two are missed. And being rather interiorially located, I suspect that might be difficult anyway.' I took a deep breath and held the gun at the ready.

'Do we have a plan?'

I considered it. 'Lean in, take a peek?'

'I've heard better, but I don't know one now.' She gave me a half-hearted smile. 'Be careful, Draygo.'

'Careful is my middle name.'

'I know it's not.'

'I'm trying to turn over a new leaf.' I look down at Rameth and tried to smile at him. It was entirely to his credit that he tried to smile back. Such an expression could be no more than a distant memory for him. 'Right.'

I turned the handle and pushed against the door, my heart hammering. It was locked of course. I banged my head against it, then handed the gun to Saunders while I rummaged through the carpet bag for my lock picking tools. It was a bit of a juggle holding Rameth and opening the lock, but at last I heard the satisfying sound of a click and we all prepared to try again.

I let Saunders hold the gun this time and grabbed the bag in my other hand instead. I figured I could always hit the dirt and she could fire over my head at whatever came up to us. My hands were getting shakier all the time. The noise if anything seemed to be getting louder as if amplified.

We burst through the door, me and Rameth going low, Saunders aiming high and we were first nonplussed by seeing no people at all. Nonetheless a cacophony pressed in tightly upon me. There was another machine attached to speakers, with dials and lights and flashing lines like a medical machine. Suddenly the noise seemed to double again and I couldn't help it, I screamed and there was a flash and Saunders shot at something and my head exploded and I lost Rameth's hand somehow as I fell and then all became blessedly black and empty for a very long time.

I won't say 'I awoke' because I didn't. I careened into consciousness with an explosion of sparks behind my eyes. I reached up to feel in vain for the axe in my skull and found my hands couldn't move. At first I thought I had fallen asleep on my arm and cut off its circulation. Instead of pins and needles, however, was simple immobility. I waited for my vision to clear. Another day of overindulgence I assumed, though there was a dull roar in my ears that seemed unusual, as if I had fallen asleep on the motorway.

Not cars though; human sounds.

The cold beneath my cheek seemed familiar: floor tiles. Yes, that was familiar enough. Then I blinked. My house had wooden floors. I hadn't felt tile floors since… when? That night in prison. Well, only for a while. I tried to open my eyes and decided closed was better, but I guessed my centre of gravity was correct in telling me I was on the floor or at least horizontal, so I tried to get up. The axe in my brain gently suggested that was madness by trying to slice through the rest of my skull.

I closed my eyes and tried to find some part of my body that worked. My ears functioned. I began to sort out the input. Then I wished I hadn't because it all came back with the screaming. I didn't really want to think about where I was but it was in my thoughts before I could stop it.

The warren. The white rabbit. The nerve centre of the place.

'Sleeping Beauty awakes!'

My eyes popped open. I groaned with the shock of it. White walls, white tiles, the machine and the man. I closed my eyes again but it wasn't going to help me any.

'Wakey, wakey, shake 'n bakey.' He prodded me with his toe. I groaned again in protest against his horrid voice if nothing else. What I really wanted was Jameson in a glass much taller than me and a whole sugar bowl of dust, and then nothing but the welcoming arms of oblivion and her consort forgetfulness.

I wouldn't get them.

'Lift him up, lads.' Rough hands did his bidding and I was hefted like a sack of potatoes onto a chair, finding my arms were tied behind me and my head lolling with the not inconsiderable pain. I wanted to be dead. After all this time, after all my dark days and black dog nights, it was the first time I could distinctly remember having that thought. But I felt it sincerely—at least for a moment or two.

'So you found my little toy,' Dockmuir said with evident pleasure. He patted the silver surface of the machine. 'Better than any drug and there's an unlimited supply.'

'Drug?' The sound of my own voice was like spikes in my head. 'Assault weapon, you mean.'

He laughed. It had the ring of genuine amusement, which made me realise just what an evil fucker he was. 'Ah, your delicate sensibilities. An acquired taste to be sure. I haven't figured out a way to bottle it, but if I can't take the mountain to a few Mohammeds, I'll bring them all to the mountain here.'

'So you don't just sell misery in the papers,' I finally rasped, trying to blink the water out of my eyes. The tears were from the physical pain, but the low-level roil of the screams surely didn't help. I thought I heard an owl's hooting; my head was severely messed up.

'The world has an appetite for pain. You should know that. It's your bread and butter.'

I blinked as I let this settle in. 'I tried to help people in my small way.' The brightness of the room stabbed my eyeballs as much as the blow to the head I assumed I'd suffered and the machine's horrible wailing.

'You were a phony trading on pain. Don't try to pretty it up. You murdered a kid and couldn't take the guilt, so you swindled even more people and lost yourself in a haze of chemicals.' He snorted with what seemed to be amusement. 'There are winners and losers and they don't change their spots.'

'I gave people comfort—'

'You gave people a drug that strung out their suffering.' He had walked right up to me. I could smell his garlicky breath as he bent over to look in my face. 'You made them hurt worse over time to feed your own nasty habit.'

'No, I—'

'You're a hustler. Instead of sex you sell hope. At least sex is natural.' He threw back his head and laughed. 'Of course you and the National Lottery, you're the same misery machine. Just a little payout now and then to keep you playing.'

I stayed silent. Guilt mostly; there was some truth in what he said. I was no hero. I was a leech, a vulture—picking over the remains, sucking on the wounds to make them larger. No wonder I wanted to die.

'It's not true,' a soft voice said from my right.

That voice: it was like a shaft of gold shining when all around was dark. Saunders!

'You're a fool,' Dockmuir said with a dismissive gesture. 'But you've thrown your lot in with him and that's your problem.'

'Sorry, Saunders,' I said twisting my neck to try to see her. She was trussed up on a chair, arms roped behind her, a shiner on her left eye that made me want to cry but with that patented Saunders look of defiance in her peepers nonetheless. I could kiss her. There was another heavy behind her and from the squeaking leather I heard, I assumed there was one behind me, too.

165

'Will you at least tell us what this machine is?' Saunders said without a tremor in her voice.

Dockmuir chuckled. 'Is this my Bond villain moment? Where I get to tell you the evil plan so you can foil it when I foolishly leave you to your fate without supervision? Sorry, not going to happen. We're going to take you one after the other and empty your head of everything useful and then dump what's left wherever there's a refuse heap high enough to hide it.'

'But don't you at least want to show us how clever you are?' I asked all innocence. Stalling for time anyway you could get it wasn't easy.

'No, I want to see how clever you are,' Dockmuir said as one of the heavies brought him my carpet bag. 'We've already got your gun, which I must say, I think my pa carried one like it in the middle of the last century.' He shook the bag and I heard the bits of the kettle clink together. I hoped he didn't figure out that was important. I had hopes we could actually use it. Anyway the orb would look more puzzling and that was bound to elicit more suspicion.

Sure enough, he pulled out the tea towel-wrapped orb and unveiled it. 'What's this?'

'You don't want to touch that,' I said trying not to over-play the panicked look.

'Why not? Oogah-boogah spirit ball?' Dockmuir laughed and bounced it up and down in his palm. The heavy beside him looked askance which I wouldn't have credited, but I suppose after all the hocus pocus around here a little agnosticism went a long way. I could feel the tension rise through my body as I tested the bindings around my hands. I wanted to be ready.

Dockmuir seemed to be measuring my response, but not finding it prohibitive, decided to test the limits. He spun on his heel and with a well-practiced bowling technique, hurled it against the laboratory-white wall of the room. The orb smashed into a million little pieces of glittering smoky quartz with a flash of sparks and a whiff of something akin to brimstone, or was it treacle? It stayed in the nose—unless it was a sensory illusion for me alone.

While Dockmuir laughed something took shape in the rubble but it wasn't anything human. I squinted at the outlines but whatever it was skittered away fairly quickly, doubtless unused to the glare. Of course the easiest place to find the shelter of shadow was under the machine.

The heavy tracked the path of my gaze and went to poke under there as Dockmuir ignored everything and went back to the bag's contents. 'A kettle? You were gasping for a cuppa?'

'You never know. When you're stuck waiting a long time, a cuppa comes in nice and handy.'

'You don't have any tea in here,' Dockmuir said, holding up the little plastic bag of my remaining dust. My heart leapt up—or some part of my anatomy—with a dread yearning for the stuff, but I knew I ought not betray the panting desire I had. I feared what he might do with it. 'What is it? Coke? Opium? Crystal? You know I've never taken drugs. Drugs are for losers.' He grinned. 'Can't go wrong with a good brownie now and then, but beer never hurt anyone.'

'No, never,' I said trying not to roll my eyes. Mostly so I could see what was going on under the machine; I heard a strange scritching noise that I was sure had to be audible but while the heavy kept an eye on me, he didn't seem to be distracted by any sound, so maybe it wasn't after all. 'A strange attitude from a pharmaceutical company CEO.'

'So,' he shook the plastic bag, 'Tell me. What has been the poison of your downward slide?'

'Something you've never heard of and don't want to know about.' I said evenly. The heavy had given up looking under the machine and gone back to an 'at ease' stance behind Dockmuir. I could still hear the scratching though. And an owl hooting. That was weird. Or an auditory hallucination. Wonderful!

'That a fact.' He looked almost curious now. 'Something of your own invention? Have you been tinkering?'

'He doesn't make it, he buys it,' Saunders offered. What a clever girl.

'Well, that was a bit too ambitious to imagine from this clapped out has-been, eh?' Dockmuir opened the bag and sniffed.

'I wouldn't do that,' I cautioned, which gained me a raised eyebrow and a frown from the mogul. 'It's powerful stuff if you're not accustomed to its... effects.'

Dockmuir snorted. 'You,' he said beckoning the heavy behind him. 'Taste this and see if you recognise it.' After a nearly imperceptible moment of hesitation, the man stepped forward and dipped a finger in the pouch. He sniffed it and then touched it to his tongue.

'No taste, no scent.' He shook his head and shrugged. The two of them looked at me.

'You wouldn't believe me if I told you.' I wondered how much effect that little bit would have on someone who'd never partook before. A few heightened senses? More vivid colours? I tried to recall my first time and seemed to recall an orgy of riotous sensations but then I had never done anything by halves. So maybe nothing at all would happen, but I could be forgiven for hoping there might be a little chaos. Then I sensed the heavy behind me stepping up. I recognised the Mancunian by his excessive use of a popular cologne.

'We can but try,' Dockmuir said with cheery brightness and a gesture to his henchman, who brought a blade to my neck.

'You don't have to torture me,' I said quickly. 'I'll tell you the truth, but you won't believe me.'

The knife at my throat didn't move. 'Well?' Dockmuir said, holding the bag aloft.

'It's fairy dust.' I said, bracing myself for the response. Indeed the knife poked into my flesh at once, the heavy not waiting for the word that I was being difficult. I felt a trickle of blood race down my neck.

'Which means—?'

'Just what it says,' I said with as much patience as possible.

'You've gone off your nut,' Dockmuir said. A quick nod and a few more cuts opened on my skin. I heard Saunders gasp. I tried not to let that panic me.

'No, straight up. I'm not kidding you. Look, you've got machines that leech away ghosts, including your own missus, so you gotta believe me when I say that dust is dust.'

That seemed to throw him off kilter a bit. 'Ghosts? What the bloody hell are you on about?'

'That ghost-sucking funnel in there,' I said with a yank of my head toward the other room. Bad idea as I could feel the blood cascading down, down, down. I realised that song was in my head again. Maybe it had been since we got here. 'The one that powers this here machine of screams.'

Was it my imagination or did the heavy behind Dockmuir start at that. He looked at the machine, but so did his boss. But he didn't look away when Dockmuir returned his gaze to me. He kept staring at the machine and started backing away.

'The eggs have slipped off your plate, I think,' Dockmuir said, shaking his head. 'This is science, not magical oogah boogah. It's taken years to develop this. I've had the finest minds in quantum electrochemistry working on this process.' Irritation crept into his tone, I noted with satisfaction.

Give me a big enough lever and I'll piss off the entire world.

'Let me guess,' I said with as much brio as I could muster with things looking hopeless and blood running in rivulets down my neck. 'You had each one working alone on one part of the machine so nobody could scoop you and know too much about it, so no one could put two and two together and suffer the effects.' I suppressed a giggle. In the midst of all this a long-forgotten Monty Python bit struggled up from the memory banks and I found myself wanting to tell Dockmuir my dog had no nose just to see if he knew the sketch.

The colonial mogul narrowed his eyes at me. 'Are you just guessing now?'

'Yes, but it's the only thing that makes sense. You don't even know what you have here, do you?'

'I know what it does, whatever your diseased mind conjures up, it's all science and effective. Look at me,' he slapped his chest. 'I've never been better, healthier, more robust.'

'Shame about the hair though,' I couldn't resist saying. He

stepped up and smacked my face himself. Vanity, thy name is balding middle-aged millionaires.

'You're a vampire,' I said, shaking my head of the stars that filled it. 'Not the blood-sucking kind, the energy sucking kind. You're bathing in other people's ghosts.' I could see the heavy starting to look around him, looking for something it seemed. Maybe he wanted to know the source of all the screaming. Or the scratching—whatever that thing was that came out of the orb, it had continued to claw away at the machine. It must have been curious, too.

With a visible effort, Dockmuir got hold of himself again. He explained to me in the tones used for very small children and idiot men, 'It's excess energy people don't need. It's screwing up their lives. I'm helping them. Clarifying them. So naturally I benefit from a natural resource they're not making any use of but I can..'

I shook my head. 'This excess 'energy'—the ghosts—don't you see removing them is harmful? We are what haunts us as much as we are what we eat and breathe. Ghosts may be screwing up our lives, but we need them to shape us into what we can be.' I looked over at Saunders and smiled. I figure that's what she had been trying to tell me all along, but I was too dust-addled to recognise it.

Saunders looked down at the floor by my feet with surprise. I glanced down to where my feet were tied to the chair to find that my feet weren't tied to the chair at all. What I had mistaken for rope on my ankle was actually Rameth, who clung to me more tightly than any knot. His big eyes met mine and I tried to smile reassuringly.

Dockmuir shrugged. 'Kill him.'

In the history of the world there could be few moments longer—and shorter—than those following two such simple words. What kings and queens heads have barked the words at countless peons only to have them repeated one final time when it was their turn on their knees? Did Mary Queen of Scots have time to draw in a breath before the axe fell? Did the surprised faces of aristocrats glimpse their own shorn necks when the guillotine slipped its bonds? How many last prayers of forgiveness, defiance or regret have sprung from lips condemned only to be cut short by the rush of blood or the explosive force of a bullet?

What did I think? Poor Rameth, at least I could lead him away somewhere if we weren't just sucked into the funnel. If we were, at least he wouldn't be alone. Poor Saunders, who wanted a story, who wanted to expose this man and his corruption, who might now get the answers about her sister's death, who never heard the words I meant to say to her. Poor Peaches, I'd let her down, I'd let her go and now at least I could apologise in person so to speak. Poor Jinxy, alone now, what would he do? I hoped someone would take in that lost soul, make him a nice cuppa now and then. Lovely Marinova: would she cry to know I was gone? Drink a measure of Lagavulin to my name so I could join the ancestors with pride? Assuming I could ever escape the infernal machine that hulked before me in order to reach that plane, that is.

But in those elastic moments between the words of condemnation and the execution thereof, something strange happened. Actually, several strange things happened. And in that way that life-changing events uncurl, everything that happened very fast in remembering seems to happen in slow motion. Maybe it's just the way our tiny brains can make sense of it—or rather the only way the horror of it all can only be borne, by separating each element as if it were discreet.

What I experienced at the time: noise, explosion, screaming, wordless sounds, pain, light, sparks, howling. Happening simultaneously, it was truly pandemonium, worse than Milton would have guessed, but the old codger was much more interested in proving a point than revealing a truth. I couldn't be certain of the sequence—there wasn't much measurable time between them, after all—but I could enumerate the events that occurred.

I owe my life, such as it is, to the heavy behind me waiting a brief second or two to secure verification of the order from Dockmuir. It stayed his hand just long enough for all the other things to happen, viz.: the frosted window behind the machine with a vent to the outside—through which, it turns out, I had heard the owl hooting—shattered due to an impatient Jinxy getting tired of waiting for me to respond to his signal, which I had forgotten, by shooting through it with his own relic of a gun. At more or less the same time, the creature who had emerged from the orb ripped loose a key panel on the underside of the machine Dockmuir used to amplify the sufferings of all the lost souls he had gathered. With the electromagnetic seal broken, the energy within expanded precipitously like a psychic thermonuclear device. The heavy who had tasted the dust had gained enough perception to collapse in a mewling ball of pain as the screams and shrieks were loosed to fill the space in a riotous cacophony the likes of which this world had not known since Pompeii.

If the second guessing of the heavy saved my neck, the shielding Auntie Vera taught me saved my mind from that assault. I was the unintentional target audience for this cataclysm. Normal(ish) humans like Dockmuir, Saunders and the other heavies could at least *feel* the explosion if not hear or see it, and naturally enough, ducked down into a defensive posture as much as they could—in Saunders' case that wasn't much, tied to the chair as she was. I was glad to have Rameth ahold of my leg as it helped ground me. As I glanced down his face radiated terror and wonder in equal parts.

He and I and all the spooks were pretty much the only ones who could see it, but I could have told the others they missed quite a show. The spirits were released like coiled springs of energy: light, faces, voices, colours blending and joining and splitting apart like a massive prog band rear projection video collage. For a moment most of them reacted to the visible boundaries of the room and rocketed around its dimensions like a fireworks display set off in a shop. Of course it was all accompanied by the horrifying shrieks, screams and then guttural cries of release as they began to recognise their freedom. But before they remembered their insubstantial natures and slipped the bonds demanded by mundane physics, I needed their help.

I summoned all my nefarious powers and drew the attention of the roiling mass. I may be the lesser for it, but glee filled me as I pointed them all at Dockmuir as the focus of their entrapment and suffering. Saunders had been right after all, as usual.

'Get him!' I said with a nod toward their torturer. The man himself, although cowed by the power he could sense if not see, had taken up a defensive posture, but there was no physical barrier—certainly not his arms crossed over his head—that could stay that unruly bunch. Some had suffered long: in death, after death, even before Dockmuir's machines sucked them down the funnel. Ghosts hang around for all kinds of reasons, but the bottom line is something has a hold on them here. Even when habit wears thin as time passes— and most ghosts have trouble telling time in this world—they cling to the thing that kept them from passing along as they ought to do.

Dockmuir ripped them all from their moorings, from the one thing that held them here. Though their bodies are beyond pain, that wrench would tear asunder whatever sense of belonging they had. In the gloomy half-lives they lead, there could be no greater suffering inflicted upon their insubstantial forms.

So they attacked him with all the power they had. For some this was actual physical blows; the spirits who had been around a while often acquired that ability. In their afterlife, there was nothing but idleness. Hobbies beyond haunting often included trying to move things or appearing to a bigger audience. The ones who'd perfected this skill buffeted their torturer with blows as strong as they could make them, some of which seemed effective indeed. So much so that the heavy formerly threatening me had gone to his boss' side and found himself suffering the same blows.

I found it hard to tell whether the heavy could also sense the intangible attacks. Dockmuir could for sure. He made a sharp keening sound as the released prisoners turned on their keeper. The swirl of them nearly obscured his head from my view and he was slumping toward the floor.

Belatedly I wondered why the heavy behind Saunders

hadn't done anything and swung back to see if he was suffering a similar distress, only to see him stretched out on the floor, bleeding from a wound in his neck. Jinxy had fired another round apparently from the window, where he was now lodged halfway through. The crazy fool had misjudged the size of the casement and now struggled uselessly. I saw signs of strain on Saunders' lovely mug, though she was looking not at Dockmuir but at the heavy on the floor. At first I thought she was maybe upset by the leakage of red from the tough guy. Eventually I realised that her eyes were on the blade he'd dropped. She glanced at me and then at the blade. I shrugged. If she were hoping that I could use the power of my mind to move it, she was going to be disappointed.

Saunders seemed to realise this. She started moving back and forth in her chair, testing how much she could move. I figured she was trying to loosen her bonds, so I was surprised when she hurled herself over. The fallen heavy broke her fall a bit but it had to hurt some anyway. What the hell was wrong with that woman? It dawned on me at last that she was trying to get the fallen blade into her bound hands, as she skittered them along the floor a good foot away from the blade.

I don't know what good it was going to do anyway if she *did* get the blade, but I tried to help anyway. 'Further away, toward me, this way.' It was difficult to find something behind you with your hands tied where you couldn't see them. If I had any psychic powers I was hoping to develop them right then. I wasn't having any luck so far.

A tug at my pant leg and I looked down. Rameth looked up at me with his puppy-sized eyes. I smiled at him and nodded. He crawled over toward Saunders and slowly pushed the blade toward her questing fingers. 'That's it. Nearly there. Go on, go on—there! She's got it.' And sure enough she did.

Of course that was only half the battle. I was terrified the whole time that Saunders would drop the blade as she sawed away at the knotted threads. The blade slipped once, almost ready to fall again but Rameth pushed it back into her fingers before it could drop. I felt a surge of joy as the ropes fell away and Saunders was free.

What a woman!

She hopped up, wiping the heavy's blood from her hands as best she could, checking for a pulse on the man anyway (such is the difference between her and I) and then with Rameth at her side, came over to release me from my chair. 'Not before time, Saunders.'

'Shut up, you idiot.'

I could have kissed her right then, but I didn't think she'd be too keen. I looked over at Dockmuir who had collapsed on the floor while the heavy crouched over him, vainly trying to defend him from an assault he could sense but not actually see. At least it distracted him for now. I kind of enjoyed the panicky look on his face. It made a nice change from the usual sneer.

To my surprise Jinx was no longer wriggling in the window. He must have decided to try another avenue of entry. At least he wasn't jammed there for the duration.

'Should we turn this thing off?' Saunders had walked over to the machine, her quick gaze sweeping its surface to suss out the details.

'We should, but we need to do something else as well.' I grabbed the carpet bag and got the spirit kettle out. 'Here, can you get some water in this?'

'You're going to make tea?' Saunders goggled at me but somehow there was a part of her that wasn't the least bit surprised.

'No, not tea—'

Before I could explain the door to the other room slammed open and a commanding voice shouted, 'Freeze!' We threw our hands up at once, not trusting to our luck today. But I was pleased to see that the squad included my old partner and even more that I could see Jinxy at the back, looking worried then relieved.

'There a chance in hell you can explain what's happened here?' Coburn said as the others collected the dazed miscreants. Dockmuir looked little more than a husk. There was nothing physically wrong with him—probably; you never know the effects of a psychic assault like that—but he had been wrung out by the spirits still dive-bombing him. When Coburn's men lifted him, he only muttered, 'Rabbit, rabbit,' in a confused way. Then his limbs trembled like he'd come over with a sudden fevre.

'We have to go.' Coburn didn't ask, but I knew he wanted me to agree.

'Look, we need to do a thing. We need to do it now. It may look stupid to you but there it is. Afterward you can haul us away, question us, lock us up, I don't care. But we just need to do this simple thing.'

Coburn looked at me with evident misgivings. All the dried blood on my neck probably didn't help much. 'How long will it take?'

'Fifteen minutes tops,' I said, hoping that was true.

'*Iba oshun sekese*,' Coburn said, wiping his hand down his face with exhaustion. 'Undoubtedly I will regret this. Do it.'

I handed the kettle to Saunders. 'Get some water in this, please. And make sure the funnel is off.' I set the burner frame on top of the machine and got the little bottle of oil out of the carpet bag. 'You wouldn't have a match would you?'

Coburn gave me a disbelieving look, then patted his pockets. I knew he still smoked those disgusting cigars when he solved something big, so I wasn't too surprised when he turned up an old Zippo in his coat pocket. 'You're going to make tea?'

'No, not tea,' I said feeling a distinct sense of déjà vu. Getting the flame to stay lit but not too scorchy ended being rather fiddly, but by the time Saunders returned with the pot, I had it going well. Rameth stared at the flame, transfixed. I hoped there wasn't any more hocus pocus required, because if I had to chant something, I was fresh out of rhymes.

The spirits still swirled around. A few had followed Dockmuir as the med techs strapped him in and rolled the stretcher away—him still muttering 'rabbit, rabbit' as if he might never stop—but most had stayed near the machine's buzz. The room was thick with them, though I suspected Rameth and I were the only ones to see it and he didn't seem to be too interested in them. He wasn't a bad kid and if I were stuck with him the rest of my natural, I decided I could maybe live with that.

The copper heated up nicely and I could hear the steam brewing despite the ethereal din. 'Right, we can probably switch off the machine now,' I said to Saunders who had watched my every move like the proverbial hawk. She reached for the big switch and turned it off. I think we all held our breath as she did so, but there wasn't an immediate effect visible even for my practiced eye.

But I could feel something in my guts gradually uncoiling and it moved like a sigh through the circling spirits. The kettle came to a boil and a plume of steam emerged from its spout. I expected it to whistle as it rose to full strength but instead the vapour began to glow with a light that was not entirely natural.

'Can you see that?' I asked Saunders, who nodded slowly. I heard Coburn swear and the uniforms with him begin to mutter. Oh, yeah: they could see it too.

I didn't know if they could see what happened next. As the glow expanded I could see insubstantial figures begin to drift toward the aperture, seeking out the gateway into the luminiferous ether. The spirit kettle was doing its work!

A thought occurred to me all of the sudden. 'Peaches! Peaches? You here, woman? Are you there?' It didn't seem likely; after all, she could have been chewed up and spat back anywhere along the insane process her ex had conjured up with his team.

Then all at once she was there in all her tacky glory and I could have kissed her just for the sheer delight of her brassy self. 'You took your time, Draygo.'

'I blame my flair for the dramatic,' I said grinning like a maniac.

'You lucky,' she said with a snort of laughter. Looking over at Saunders she said, 'I'm amazed you put up with this one for so long. You deserve some kind of medal, I'm sure.'

Saunders looked dazed and laughed kind of half-heartedly. 'Am I really seeing her?'

'She don't believe her own eyes.' Peaches looked down at herself. 'I am getting rather thin, innit the truth?'

'Svelte as hell,' I agreed. 'Oh, but before you go, can I ask a favour?'

'Considering your success in slaying the white rabbit, I say yeah. What's your pleasure?'

I put a hand on Rameth's insubstantial shoulder. 'Could you shepherd this young lad to safety?' I looked down at him to see if he were willing and found a happy grin stretching his face. He took Peaches' offered hand and stepped away from me. 'Thank you, son. I'm sorry I took your life and I'm more sorry I held you here. Go in peace.'

'I'll see he makes it through,' Peaches said, leaning over to kiss me on the cheek, her lips a brush of cloud-thin mist.

And they stepped through the light as if it were nothing and I tried to swallow the lump in my throat and pretend I wasn't crying.

I don't know how long it took all together. Half an hour, maybe less, and the room was just a room, though a little more humid than when we started. I blew out the light under the kettle and set it gingerly in the carpet bag. The water in the kettle itself had boiled away to nothing. It seemed to have taken the weight off my shoulders, too. I probably looked like death warmed over with beans on the side, but inside I felt like the sharp end of a lion's roar.

I picked up the carpet bag and turned to Coburn to tell him I was done just in time to see Saunders pick up the chair she had been tied to, lift it over her head and slam it into the dials of the machine. The squeal of the metal legs on the glass and steel made us all wince.

'Sorry,' she said with a shrug.

How could you not love a woman like that?

Coburn herded us out past the funnel machine, upon which similar violence had been visited. I glanced at Saunders, but she was staring off into the distance with a look of complete innocence.

Maybe it was Jinxy anyway.

The ride to the station stayed quiet, all of us lost in our own thoughts. Saunders was between me and Jinx which seemed appropriate enough. We duly made our statements under Coburn's watchful eye. I noticed that he elided a lot of details from the report. I had no idea how he was going to account for it.

'Life is full of mystery,' he murmured as he took Saunders' signature. My former partner was showing his magnanimous side. Of course he and the unit had never much cared for Dockmuir's empire of dirty cop headlines and law-and-order hysterics. The tabs whipped up a lot of useless frenzy.

But you could have knocked me over with a very tiny feather when Coburn gruffly ordered a uniform to drive us home. I had a feeling I should stop off at an off-license to buy a lotto ticket or at the very least drop by the Silver Wheel and let Marinova know the good news. Truth was I was exhausted beyond my capacity to do anything but find my bed. Jinx and Saunders apparently agreed, each heading off to their own corners as soon as we came through the door.

I was pleased to see Saunders didn't head back to her own place. Jinx was too. 'You done good, Jinxy.' I said with a sense of happy gratitude. He shrugged, but I saw his little smile. 'See you in the morning.'

I stumbled toward my room loosening buttons and yawning. A glance in the mirror over my sink suggested I would look a considerable wreck tomorrow, but I couldn't be arsed to do more than wash off what was left of the caked blood from my neck. It felt as if a month or more had passed since I last left the house. I fell into the bed as if into a grave but for once I didn't have any desire to assuage the aches with a shake of dust. Of course, not having any I couldn't really do much about that. There were plenty of other medicinals at hand, but the urge was not upon me.

I slept without dreams.

Awaking disoriented, I wondered briefly where I was. Home somehow looked different. I blinked and out of habit reached for the nightstand beside the bed, though my hand stopped before it reached the drawer. Habits, they get you.

Then I saw the key lying on the stand. Old, rusty, ornate: I realised as I picked up the key to turn it over in my hands that the filigree pattern of the bow looked like an owl's head. After all this time, it looked like Auntie Vera finally had a present for me.

I could smell bacon cooking, so I threw on some jeans and buttoned a soft shirt and headed to the kitchen, bouncing the key in my hand like a lucky charm. 'I hope you got that kettle boiling, Jinx,' I said as I barged into the kitchen.

Saunders looked up as she dropped her dish in the sink. 'Morning,' she said, turning her head away quickly.

I wasn't to be put off. 'Look what I've got.' I held the key up for their inspection.

Jinx shrugged and shook his head. Saunders gave me the one eyebrow. 'Key to the castle?'

'It's the key to the garden in the square! I thought Auntie Vera had lost it years ago. But there it was on the nightstand when I woke up. Can't beat that with a stick, as they say. I say we have a fine picnic lunch today.'

Jinx nodded with a smile of pure pleasure. He knew a winning idea when it plopped right in front of him.

Saunders gave me a half smile. 'I have to head out. In fact I was just off now.' She bustled around, giving a kiss to the top of Jinxy's head, then passing me by with a flushed smile.

I followed her to the door. 'You can't run off now.'

'There's going to be so much email piled up, to say nothing of the actual mail, too. I can't run away from my life for as long as you can. I have deadlines.'

'Let them hang for one more day. You deserve it. Have a picnic. See the sights.'

She was moving so fast, she had already opened the door before she stopped for a moment to think up a reply. The morning light gave her face a sheen of gold, yet it was only gilding the lily. A slight blush burnished her cheeks and took my breath away for a moment.

Then the ginger cat walked in between her legs like it owned the place and sat looking up at me expectantly. 'See, we get all kinds here.'

Saunders gave me a look I couldn't parse. 'You see to your spooks, I'll see to my email and what not.' Then almost as if she were hoping it wouldn't happen, she leaned over and kissed me.

I managed to resist the urge to go all Groucho Marx on her and swing her into some kind of swooning dip, but I was more than ready to go there myself.

She turned and walked swiftly away down the street without looking back once. The ghost of her smile lingered in my mind. I bounced the key in my hand, feeling as if I were slightly dusted and walking on air. I looked down at the ginger cat and gave her a wink. 'She'll be back.'

~The End~

25028629R00107

Printed in Great Britain
by Amazon